DEADLY CARGO

JODIE BAILEY

LOVE INSPIRED SUSPENSE

INSPIRATIONAL ROMANCE

Special thanks and acknowledgment are given to Jodie Bailey
for her contribution to the Alaska K-9 Unit miniseries.

LOVE INSPIRED® SUSPENSE
INSPIRATIONAL ROMANCE

ISBN-13: 978-1-335-55449-9

Recycling programs
for this product may
not exist in your area.

Deadly Cargo

Love Inspired
22 Adelaide St. West, 40th Floor
Toronto, Ontario M5H 4E3, Canada
www.Harlequin.com

Printed in U.S.A.

For he hath said, I will never leave thee, nor forsake thee.
So that we may boldly say, The Lord is my helper,
and I will not fear what man shall do unto me.
—*Hebrews* 13:5–6

To Caroline,
You were in my heart as I wrote this.
You are so very strong, and I'm honored to call you my friend.

ONE

She would beat that storm to the airstrip even if it killed her.

Jasmine Jefferson drew her lips between her teeth and glanced out the right window of her twin-engine aircraft, where dark banks of clouds dumped undulating sheets of rain that already obscured the horizon.

Check that. Failure to beat the storm might be what actually killed her.

It would definitely be ironic if she died doing a job she'd taken under the identity the government had given her in order to protect her from a murderer.

She hated irony.

A sudden gust shoved the Twin Otter sideways. Jasmine fought the urge to grip the yoke tighter and glanced at her gauges. With a slight nudge, she drew the plane back on course and peered out the front window as she raised the airspeed to account for the variation in wind gusts. She should be able to see the small landing strip at Nemeti, where the "ground crew" was waiting for the cargo she was flying in from Fairbanks.

Landing was going to be tough today. Doubly so because the load she'd picked up this morning was heavier than usual after a freak summer storm had leveled half of a small survival camp forty-five minutes from the remote airstrip. A combination of ferocious wind and flooding rain had nearly wiped out two cabins, and they had to rebuild fast, before the beast of winter roared in.

In this part of Alaska, August was the start of the change. It might be in the sixties today, but the first snowfall was coming up quickly. "Termination snow," when the summer tourist season ended and Alaska winter set in.

Jasmine pulled her head from side to side to stretch out her tight neck muscles. She had to land this plane and land it well, not only for her survival, but also for the sake of those who counted on her to get supplies to them.

Out the front window, the landscape rested flat between the mountains, greener than most people imagined Alaska could be.

There. The airstrip stood out as a straight brown slash in the summer-green brush. At least she didn't have to land off-airport here. With the sudden storm closing in fast, a brush landing was a creature she wouldn't want to tame. She spoke into her radio. "Nevada five-seven-five-xray-romeo. I'm about two minutes out and coming in at forty-two knots. Looks like the mountains to the east are blocking the wind on the runway. Confirm?"

"Confirmed. We have the wind sock up for verification." Maya Carter's voice in her ear was calm, but it held an unusual tension. The owner of the small frontier airstrip was usually chatty and friendly, even in the most dire situations.

Her curt demeanor now drew Jasmine's eyebrows together. "Anything else I need to know?"

The radio was silent for long seconds. "No. You've handled worse. You'll be fine."

There it was again. A brusque answer. No cordiality. No teasing about the flight. No "can't wait to have some girl talk" gab. As the lone female on the small airstrip made up of a dirt runway, a small office/maintenance building and a separate locked cargo shed, Maya was usually ready and waiting for Jasmine's visits.

As another gust shook the plane, Jasmine jerked her attention back to the controls. This wasn't the time to worry about what had put her friend on edge. This was the time to set this Twin Otter down safely. With another glance at the gauges, she turned her nose into the wind, crabbing sideways to keep her flight path centered on the runway. The transition from wind to relative calm was coming up as soon as she got the mountain range to her right, and she had to be ready to adjust for the sudden decrease in winds. The drop in wind speed could drop the plane like a boulder if she wasn't ready.

She upped her airspeed to compensate. With one eye on her gauges and the other on the mountains, she finessed the controls until—

With a rush that brought her stomach into her throat, the plane jerked and threatened to plummet belly first as the mountains blocked the wind. But she was ready. She'd flown this route enough times to know its peculiarities, even in a storm. Reaching up, she adjusted the throttle down to control her altitude, and straightened up slightly to side slip the landing, using the rudder to align the nose with the airstrip's imaginary center line. Then she drifted off center and banked the plane slightly to stay on her ground track, adjusting the left rudder and the right aileron.

"I saw that." The radio opened with Maya's voice. "Nice job."

Once again, the tone was different than the words. Something was definitely off. Jasmine held her line and scanned the airport, looking for trouble. Had someone crashed? Tried to rob the airstrip? Been busted flying in illegal drugs?

That last one wasn't out of the realm of possibility. The number of overdoses in the remote villages had spiked over the past few months, and state law enforcement had dug in to investigate. Kramer Anderson out of Sea-Bush Air had been raided on landing in Sitka recently, after a tip indicated he was carrying fentanyl and oxycodone in his cargo.

He wasn't. But the incident and several others like it in previous weeks had Alaska's bush pilots on edge and even eyeing one another with suspicion. With cargo largely ferried in and out of the frontier by plane, the odds were high that one of them was up to something illegal.

But today, nothing seemed out of place on the airstrip. A couple of people stood outside the small maintenance shed, but they were likely trying to seek shelter from the coming storm. Only Maya, her husband, Dean, and their oldest son maintained the small airstrip, and it wasn't out of the ordinary for them to be waiting when Jasmine landed.

She reduced power and brought the flaps down, checking her gauges as she scanned the end of the runway, judging where to round out. The right wheel settled down, and she increased back pressure on the yoke to keep the nose wheel from slamming into the ground. She didn't level the wings until all three wheels were safely on the ground. Sagging in her seat, Jasmine exhaled and coasted down the small dirt airstrip toward the metal buildings.

A torrent of rain unleashed as she stopped the plane as close to the cargo shed as she could and then cast up a quick prayer. *Thank you, Lord, for another safe trip.* She'd beat the weather.

They could unload when the rain stopped. Hopefully, Maya was in a better mood than she seemed, because Jasmine would probably be at Nemeti for an hour or so until the squall line passed. A cup of coffee and girl talk sure sounded like it would hit the spot.

She braked the plane and ran through the procedure to power down as Maya's husband, Dean, set the chocks beneath the wheels and retreated toward the cargo shed.

Jasmine pulled a ball cap on her head to combat the rain, then hesitated with her hand on the door handle. *Odd.* Dean usually hung out nearby and waited for her to deplane.

She took a deep breath. Likely the weather had driven him back under cover. She'd spent two years looking over her shoulder, ever since she'd wrapped up her testimony in court and moved on to her new life. Today wasn't the day to start getting suspicious all over again. Shoving open the door, she turned and climbed down to the ground, her back hunched against the driving rain.

Her feet sank into mud. She prayed the airstrip wouldn't be too waterlogged for her to take off again. Missing her other two deliveries would throw her off schedule, but it wouldn't be the first time she'd had to bunk on Maya's couch at the—

"State troopers! Jasmine Jefferson, place your hands behind your head, turn around slowly and get on your knees!"

Her heart pounded painfully from a rush of adrenaline, then seemed to stop beating entirely. She froze. *What?*

"Do it now!" Behind her, the sounds of splashing feet drew near.

She obeyed, lacing her hands against soaking wet hair at the back of her neck as rain stung her face. Slowly, she turned.

Two unfamiliar men approached her, shadows in the driving rain. Their features were hard to make out, but one thing was certain.

Each one of them held a gun.

And each gun was aimed squarely at her.

Alaska state trooper Will Stryker kept his aim steady, even as wind-lashed rain slapped him in the face and poured from the brim of his cover. Beside him, his K-9 partner stood near his left calf, stalwart in the sudden relentless weather. The border collie's fur hung heavy with rain, but Scout stood firm, well trained and ready to work.

And work he would. As soon as they detained Jasmine Jefferson, Will would set Scout loose inside the airplane to search out any drugs the pilot was ferrying into the remote airstrip at Nemeti.

Several anonymous tips in the previous weeks had been bogus, and each time they came up empty it had demoralized them both. Today *had* to be different.

Hopefully, this would be the day they took down a link in a burgeoning supply chain before more people overdosed on the fentanyl and oxycodone that had begun to creep its way into the area.

He kept his weapon leveled on the pilot as she turned, the ball cap she wore doing little to shield her face from the rain. Her eyes met his. Far from appearing defiant or guilty, Jasmine Jefferson appeared pale and terrified, as though she might drop to the mud at any moment.

For a brief second, his heart went out to her, but he shook off the pity, burned by the memory of too many liars who had worn that same expression. He wasn't buying her fear. Their tipster had claimed she was armed and would do anything to protect her illegal cargo.

Will couldn't take any chances. He barked an order to the trooper beside him as he holstered his sidearm. "Tell her why we're here. Check her for weapons, then take her inside and detain her there until we've searched the plane." After the other trooper moved forward and secured the suspect, Will stepped closer, with Scout keeping pace alongside him.

As he passed Ms. Jefferson, his eyes locked on hers again, even though he'd had every intention of passing her right by without a second glance.

She swallowed so hard he could see the motion in her neck. Rain streamed down her face, and it seemed to be mixed with panic-stricken tears from her wide eyes. "Why?"

Will's chest seized with her one pleading word. There was pain there. Real fear. Fear that seemed to have nothing to do with her current situation. She looked as though she thought her life was at stake. Reflexively, he started to give her an answer that would calm her, but then he stopped. He had a job to do. Comforting a criminal wasn't his responsibility. The other trooper who'd met him here would handle the explanation. Will had different duties to attend to.

Even though the expression on her face hit him square in the gut.

He glanced down at Scout, who stood by his side, looking up at him expectantly.

Will's eyes narrowed. Odd. His partner wasn't paying one iota of attention to Jasmine Jefferson. If she'd been anywhere near drugs, Scout's super sniffer would be all over it, and he'd be doing his happy little "I succeeded now give me a treat" dance. But the dog wasn't alerting. He merely waited patiently for his next command.

No. Will couldn't base her innocence on that. If her person was clean, that only meant she hadn't loaded the drugs onto the plane. Nothing else.

With the help of the man on the grounds crew, Will opened the cargo door of the Twin Otter and hoisted Scout inside. The cargo area was the typical smaller size of a bush plane hauling supplies. This wouldn't take long. Within a couple of minutes, he'd have his proof *and* his drug runner. One more way to sweep death and addiction off the streets...or out of the skies, in this case.

He nearly cracked a smile at his humor. Instead, he gave Scout a quick rub on the back of his neck. "You ready?" He swept his hand toward the back of the plane. *"Search."*

With an excited tail wag, Scout went to work. His nose twitched at crates, bags and boxes without pause.

He continued down the narrow aisle and trotted back, downcast at finding nothing. For Scout, this was a game. The scent of various drugs had been placed inside his favorite toy during training until he associated those specific odors with play and reward.

But now? The border collie was disappointed.

Will shook his head, glanced at the small shed that served as an office, where the other trooper had led Jasmine Jefferson, then gave Scout the command again.

Without hesitation, his partner obeyed.

Once again, he came back dejected.

As he gave his faithful partner a quick head rub, Will sympathized with the border collie's disappointment. He'd hoped to end this day with a bust, saving the lives of whoever was waiting for those drugs at the end of the supply line. Instead, he'd come up empty. Again.

Been made to play the fool. Again.

"Didn't find anything, did you." It wasn't a question. Footsteps sloshed up slowly behind him as the rain began to slacken, falling straight down instead of zinging like horizontal water darts. Dean Carter, the airport's owner and chief mechanic, stepped up beside Will and rested his hand on the fuselage of the plane. "I told you Jasmine wasn't hauling drugs. She's as straight arrow as they come. And one of the nicest people you'll ever meet."

Will helped Scout down from the plane, clipped a leash to his harness, then turned to the other man. "*Nice* doesn't mean a thing. Unload the cargo into the shed as normal, and I'll have Scout check one more time." He stepped back, prepared to supervise, to make triple certain that no one took anything off that plane and squirreled it away somewhere before Scout could have another pass at it.

Dean quirked an eyebrow and waved his son over to help. "Can't say *you're* one of the nicest people I've ever met." He turned his back on Will and pulled himself into the plane.

The comment stung, but he shook it off. He wasn't here to make friends. Someone was contributing to the high addiction rates in the remote villages of Alaska, and they had to be stopped.

Will was going to do whatever it took to find them, even if everyone from Nome to Juneau considered him to be their number one enemy.

TWO

Even though the small office was warm, Jasmine was soaking wet and freezing cold. It felt like an earthquake rattled her from somewhere deep inside, shaking her limbs and knocking her teeth together. Perched on the edge of a worn leather sofa, she wrapped her arms around her middle and stared at her feet.

Near the door, the trooper who'd escorted her into the building stood sentry. He'd informed her that an anonymous tip about opioids had led them to her plane, and now he stood guarding her.

Guarding. Her. As though she was the criminal.

Jasmine shook her head. What did the trooper think she was going to do? Sprout wings and fly through the ceiling? Attack him with her baseball cap? She was shaking so hard she doubted her knees would even let her stand, let alone fight her way out of the small plywood and metal building.

If they only knew who she was, how she'd sacrificed her identity to testify against the types of criminals they now hunted, they'd—

"I'm sorry, Jas." Across the room behind a small desk that acted as a customer counter, Maya had been watching her since they entered the building. "I told them you wouldn't carry drugs. Dean tried to tell them, too. But that guy out there, Trooper Stryker? He wouldn't listen."

Jasmine lifted her head. Water ran off the top of her cap and slid down her neck, trailing along her spine like a cold finger of fear. "You did what they asked you to do, but thanks for trying. Have you reached out to Keith and Darrin?" Her bosses, brothers and owners of Kesuk Aviation, would want to know about both the allegations and the delay in deliveries.

Well, technically they already knew, since the trooper at the door had also informed her that the "aircraft's owners" had given permission for the search. Jasmine cringed. What were they thinking about her? This could cost her the job she loved. And for someone in WITSEC, finding another one was never without risk.

"I did. They're confident you're clean, but Keith said he'd head up here if you need him."

"Not yet." Jasmine gripped her stomach tighter and wished she could see the airstrip, but the trooper blocked the door. "Most of the cargo comes to us already packed, and I supervise loading. What if…" Shaking her head, she studied the plywood ceiling. *Lord, please don't let someone have smuggled something onto my plane. Please don't let me land in jail.*

It wasn't merely the *thought* of prison that terrified her. Because for her, going into the system could be a matter of life and death.

The door swung open and the trooper who'd been leading the charge entered, a dripping wet border collie at his side.

He said something under his breath to the trooper standing guard, then turned to Maya. "Thank you for your help." When he faced Jasmine, his dark brown eyes flickered with something warm but unreadable. Just as quickly, they went cold again. "Your plane's clean. I'm sorry for the inconvenience."

He pivoted on his heel with a swift hand motion to the dog and started to leave.

All of the pent-up fear and anxiety—two years' worth—exploded in Jasmine's gut, as sudden and violent as the squall that had nearly swept her plane from the sky. "That's it?" She rocketed up from the couch, her feet rooted to the floor, but her hands flew with all of the Italian blood her grandmother had gifted her. "You're *sorry*? For the *inconvenience*? I don't think so."

At the door, the trooper's back stiffened, his shoulders a straight line beneath his navy blue rain jacket. His head tilted slightly as his chin rose.

"You aimed a gun at me." She pointed at the couch. "You made me sit here and sweat, absolutely terrified that a package someone loaded onto my plane might have something in it that I didn't know about. What if that had happened? Where would I be right now?" She stepped closer and huffed out a breath. "Trooper Stryker? That's your name, right? You owe me so much more than a *sorry*. You *and* your dog."

For a long moment, he stared out the door and across the airstrip as the sky outside began to brighten. The only movement was the rise and fall of his shoulders as he breathed. He was probably going to walk out and leave her to her righteous indignation.

But then, with one deep exhale, he dismissed the other trooper, who ducked out the door and disappeared.

Dude was probably grateful to get out of her heated presence.

Finally, Trooper Stryker turned toward her, though he didn't quite meet her eye. He aimed a finger at the opposite end of the couch from where she stood. "Okay if I sit?"

"Fine."

He was taller than she'd initially thought, slim and fit. When he swept his hat off his head, he smoothed back damp, dark hair that probably tended to curl when it was longer.

Jasmine shifted her attention to the dog at his side. The well-groomed collie sure was cute. He settled at his handler's feet and rested his chin on his front paws. His longish hair was still wet, even though he'd likely already had a good shake before they came in. While the trooper might be on her bad side, his dog certainly didn't deserve to be.

Jasmine looked over her shoulder at Maya. "Is there a spare towel around so we can dry the dog?"

"I can probably find something in the shed." She pushed away from the desk and headed for the back door with a silent *You okay?*

Jasmine nodded and looked down at the dog as Maya left the room.

"His name's Scout." The trooper's voice was gentler this time.

Jasmine ignored his attempt to offer an olive branch. "He looks for narcotics?"

"He's a trained sniffer, yes." Trooper Stryker cleared his throat and sat back on the couch. "You're right. I didn't need to be so short with you. And while the apology was a little curt, I promise it was sincere. There's a lot of frustration right now, and it shouldn't have come out on you."

"I would never, *ever* transport drugs. I love the people out here. Their safety is why I do what I do, why I fly in these conditions." She waved her hand toward the door where the sun now shone as though a rogue squall hadn't just savagely beaten them. "Never in a million years would I haul drugs in here and cause that kind of harm. That's not love. That's the opposite. It's selfish greed."

"I understand." He exhaled loudly. "But half an hour ago, all I had was a tip that Jasmine Jefferson was flying in narcotics and that she was armed and willing to do battle. I don't know you. In fact, before today, I'd never even heard your name. And in my line of work, I can't afford to assume everyone is kind and loving." His fingers drummed on the worn arm of the couch. "That's how troopers get killed."

"And from my side? It's not every day I have guns aimed at me." If only she could say she'd *never* had one aimed at her. Swallowing hard, she forced herself to hold his gaze. "See it from my point of view."

"Hence the apology. The *sincere* apology." He slid forward on the sofa and rested his elbows on his knees, clasping his hands as he leaned forward and stared out the open door. "Actually, maybe you can help me."

"You want me to help you? After how today went down?" Jasmine chuckled, but it was bitter, and it snapped off in the middle. She sounded like a shrew. Like someone who didn't appreciate law enforcement when, in all honesty, she probably appreciated them more than most. While this guy had definitely started off on an incredibly wrong foot, and her fear had set fire to her anger, she knew she needed to dial it back. "I guess it's my turn to toss the *sorry* out there."

"Believe it or not, I understand." He flashed a quick grin, but it didn't last. "It's hard on me and on Scout when we think we have a lead and it all falls apart. I want to take down the bad guys who are running drugs to these people. Right now, all we have are tips, and we have to follow every single one of them that is credible. The one about you was specific enough to be credible."

"You got an anonymous tip about my plane, just like Kramer Anderson and the others."

"We did. Only the others didn't indicate weapons the way yours did."

"So you want to catch the smugglers so badly that you launch at every tip like a bottle rocket?" Somehow, remembering that she wasn't in this alone, that Kramer had been the victim, too, eased her ire. "So what help do you need from me?"

"*Bottle rocket?* That's a good one. And we only launch if there's enough specific information to make the threat credible. If we ran after every anonymous tip, we'd never get any work done." This time, he turned his head when he smiled at her. It changed everything about his face. Made him appear—

Jasmine looked away. Handsome or not, she had no reason to be noticing him.

Stryker stood and paced the room as though he was ready to be moving forward on his investigation rather than talking to her. "Over the past couple of months, we've had a spike in overdoses on the frontier to the northwest of the city. At some of the villages and outposts."

Jasmine had heard as much, and she'd felt helpless to do anything about it. She'd lain awake at nights praying for the addicted and the hopeless.

"Scout and I have been called in to head up the investigation. It's isolated out here. There's no regular law enforcement. Even the trooper backing me up today just happened to be nearby. There's no easy way in, so if we can cut off the supply chain at the head, then—"

"Then you can help keep everybody safe." The last of Jasmine's ire fizzled. While the trooper might have been unnecessarily abrupt, it was clear the safety of the people she served was paramount. "How did you get out here?"

"Helicopter. They're waiting for me to call them to pick me up." He pulled his phone from a clip on his belt, flicked the screen and read something, then tapped a few more times.

The silence stretched long. Was she free to go out and get the plane ready for her next hop? Or did she have to wait to be released? She was behind schedule and had two more stops to make. Every second the trooper spent reading his texts, more time ticked off the clock.

Seeming to sense her tension, Scout looked up then trotted over and rested his chin on Jasmine's knee. His big brown eyes hinted at a bit of mischief. Instinctively, Jasmine scratched behind the dog's damp ears. "Maya will get you dried off soon, buddy."

At her words, the trooper tucked his phone away. Something in his expression had hardened, but it seemed to pass quickly as he watched her and his dog. "About my helicopter ride back to Fairbanks... I have a better idea, if you're game for it. It has to do with what I mentioned earlier. A way you could help me."

Jasmine pulled her hand from Scout's head, and the dog settled at the trooper's feet with a contented sigh. "You want me to fly you around." The thought of spend-

ing the rest of the day cooped up with this guy in her
tiny cockpit brought on even more stress.

And honestly? She sneaked a peek at him. From the
top of his recently trimmed hair to the soles of his damp
but highly polished shoes, he was buttoned-up blue uniform. Not the type to run around in the wild.

But she would help the people out here any way she
could. "Did you offload my whole plane?"

"Dean and I did, but he said you'd have to reload
some of the cargo since this was your first stop."

"I have two more stops today, and now I'm running
behind. If you help me reload, then you can hitch a
ride with me. I'll get you to Fairbanks by the end of the
day." She stood, resigned to the company of a man she
wasn't sure she could tolerate. She cast a quick look at
his partner. At least the dog was cute. "But Scout gets
the copilot's seat. You can ride in the back."

While Jasmine finished securing cargo and doing
her preflight, Will led a now-leashed Scout around to
the back of the building for a short walk before they
hopped aboard for what would likely be a tense flight.

If he was quick and made sure no one managed to
get within earshot, he had time to call Eli Partridge,
the Alaska K-9 Unit's tech whiz, to clarify the text Eli
had sent earlier. If it was real, they might have a bigger mess on their hands than Will had ever considered.

Eli picked up before the phone even rang once.
"You're slow today. I thought I'd hear from you ten
minutes ago while that text was still hot on my fingers."

"I couldn't answer right away. I had Jasmine Jefferson sitting right beside me. Are you sure your intel
is right?"

"It's a cursory search, but I'm already digging deeper." Clicks and taps came through the line, evidence that the other man was multitasking as usual. "What I passed through to you is a little smelly to me. Jasmine Jefferson's online history is thin. She has no digital trail at all. I mean, given her age and other demographic factors, it's slightly suspicious to me that she's not on social media. No online dating profiles either. I was able to tag one email address, and that seems to be all she has."

"Did you track the email address? See what sites it's been used on?"

"I went as far as I could, but I didn't find any usernames that link to it."

So Jasmine was hiding. But there were a lot of people in Alaska who were off the grid. In fact, his unit was working a case now that delved into that survivor mentality. "Lots of people stay away from social media."

"But rarely without a reason. And she has a nice, clean record that doesn't indicate any motive as to why she'd want to be invisible."

That was true. He'd read her file on the helo flight up to Nemeti. Her schooling, previous jobs and training held nothing out of the ordinary. Other than a handful of parking tickets in Kansas and a speeding ticket in Illinois, there was nothing to blemish a spotless record. It made something at the back of his neck itch, although he couldn't explain why. Hearing Eli say the same only heightened his wariness. "I'll do some talking to her today. I'm flying out with her on the rest of her stops and will be back in Fairbanks later this evening."

The tapping stopped. "Watch your back. Her plane

might have been clean today, but that doesn't mean it's *always* clean."

"Believe me, I know. Few people are as honest as they appear to be." He'd fallen victim to that himself, and the fact that he'd been fooled still made his stomach clench.

"Jefferson could be hiding from someone she double-crossed. She could be trying to steer clear of a jealous ex. Or she could simply be a very boring, very private, very innocent bush pilot."

Will doubted that. "Keep digging for me and see what you come up with."

"Right now I'm knee-deep into some new intel on the Missing Bride case, but I'm running Jasmine's driver's license photo to see if we get a hit on facial rec. That takes time, though."

Will glanced behind him. Jasmine was chatting with Dean, far enough away to be out of earshot. "What's the latest on the bride case?" Five months earlier, oil heiress Violet James had vanished after someone murdered the tour guide for her wedding party's trek into Chugach State Park. Her best friend had been shoved off a cliff and nearly killed. While Violet had been the initial suspect, intel now pointed squarely at her fiancé and his best man, who were on the run. The team hoped to apprehend the two men and locate Violet before anyone else was killed.

"Just following up on some leads coming in from Anchorage, since they've been spotted around there. ATM cameras, traffic cams, that kind of thing. So far, there's nothing." Eli exhaled heavily. "Anyway, I'm headed out on my lunch break to visit with my godmother, so you might not get anything from me before you get back to Fairbanks."

Will let his head drop against the green metal siding of the small shed. He should have led with asking about Eli's godmother. She was dying of cancer and had asked if the team could locate her son, a survivalist somewhere in the Alaska wilderness. So far, they'd been unable to locate any trace of him or his family, and the strain weighed heavily on Eli. "How is she?"

"Not good. I'm guessing we're at the point that hospice is our next step." Eli's voice was heavy.

Will couldn't make it better, but sure wished he could. "I'm sorry, man. As soon as I'm done up here, I'll put some extra focus on your situation. I know the clock's ticking."

"Thanks. And I'll forward you anything else I find on Ms. Jefferson. Stay safe."

"You, too." Will killed the call and shoved his phone into its holster. He edged closer to the corner of the building and watched Jasmine chat with Dean on the muddy dirt. Her brown hair escaped her ball cap in ten different directions. While her stance was relaxed, her eyes were hidden behind dark sunglasses. Everyone seemed to think she was perfect, but what if she wasn't? What exactly was she hiding? Or *who* was she hiding from?

It was risky to fly off into the frontier alone with her, but she'd be foolish to try something when the whole world knew he and Scout were with her.

He looked down at his partner, who sat by his left foot. "Well, buddy, are you ready to fly?"

As if he understood, Scout jumped to his feet, prepared for action. He was going to need a serious brushing when they got back to the hotel tonight. Probably a bath, too. That rain shower hadn't done his long coat any favors.

"Let's get moving, Trooper!" Jasmine's voice floated across the space between them. She strode toward the plane, probably anxious to go.

Hoping she was joking with him about having to ride in the cargo area, Will joined her in the front of the plane and secured Scout slightly behind and between their seats. He buckled himself in and watched as she finished her preflight preparations. Then she gave him a quick lecture on passenger behavior, including the need to stay silent during takeoff and landing.

Will situated his headset for the flight. After takeoff, he settled back for a few minutes to watch the terrain go by beneath them. While he spent most of his time in and around Anchorage and other cities, he frequently found himself in more remote areas. Two of his most recent cases had found him chasing down poachers with Trooper Poppy Walsh and her Irish wolfhound, Stormy, near Glacier Bay National Park and taking out a theft ring with Trooper Helena Maddox and her Norwegian elkhound, Luna, near Denali.

Still, Alaska never ceased to amaze him, and this remote area north of Fairbanks was one he hadn't had the opportunity to see before. The state had so many different personalities, depending on where you decided to put your foot down. From the dangerously wild and untamed to the everyday civilized and modern, Alaska was a land that could make your head spin.

Jasmine navigated the plane over a flat green landscape sliced by rivers and streams. The mountains rose a short distance away to his right, stark and capped by snowy white glaciers. He could travel this state for years and never see it all. From the air, it was even more stunning than it was on the ground.

While he studied the land below, the quiet tension in the plane grew even heavier. Silence was often his best weapon, a simple way to keep suspects off their guard. He had no doubt Jasmine was hiding something. He could practically feel the stress radiating off her.

Still, even he could only take the quiet for so long. "We're coming up on aurora season, aren't we?" His voice sounded strange as it filtered through the mic and back into the headset, slightly nasally. When he was a kid and had watched TV shows, that kind of voice had sounded of adventure. In a way, it still did.

Reaching up, Jasmine adjusted the throttle then dropped her hand to the yoke again. "Any day now."

"Ever seen it from up here?"

She eyed him through her sunglasses. "I'm not a fan of flying at night. Straight instrument flying isn't a lot of fun. And with the mountains, there's too much chance of a controlled flight into terrain."

"A *what*?"

"A crash." She faced the front and shrugged. "I'm sure the light shows are pretty, but you won't be seeing them with me. It won't get fully dark until about 10:30. We'll be back in Fairbanks by then. And even if we weren't, we're on the border of the season starting. Might not get a show for a few more days or even into next week."

Now that he had her talking, he needed to get her relaxed, then catch her off guard with the questions he really wanted to ask. "I've only lived here a few years. Alaska still amazes me. It's a whole other world."

"Where'd you come from?"

"Kansas." Actually, he'd made the move from Minnesota, but given that her background check said she used to live in Kansas, he wanted to search for recognition.

Her fingers seemed to tighten on the yoke, but then she nodded. "I lived there once. It was a long time ago."

Interesting. The parking tickets in her file were only about four years old. Anger and pride threatened to rise up and do battle with his common sense. There was nothing he hated more than being lied to. *Nothing.*

He'd been warned more than once that his past sometimes threw a cloud over his judgment, that he was too suspicious, too cynical. He didn't think that was necessarily a bad thing in his line of work.

Trying to shake off his irritation, Will dropped his left hand and reached back to scratch Scout's chin. He had to keep his voice level, his questions focused, but it was time to move in for some answers. "How long have you been flying in Alaska?"

"About two years." Jasmine made a show of studying the gauges in front of her. "I love it. Wouldn't want to do anything else."

"And before that?"

She glanced at him. Something in her expression was off, but she turned toward her side window before he could read what it was. "I flew freight for an international shipping company. Regional hops from their main hub in Illinois out to surrounding states."

Just like her background check said. "Where'd you get your pilot's license?"

"I'm sorry," she snapped, much like she had back at the airstrip. This time, though, there was more fear than anger behind the words. "Why am I being interrogated? My plane was clean. I'm not the smuggler you're looking for. I'm doing you a favor letting you fly a couple of hops today. If you'd stop focusing on me, maybe you'd find who you're really looking for."

Knowing they'd be landing before too long, Will calculated his next move. She couldn't get away from him right now. Wouldn't crash the aircraft unless she was truly desperate, which she didn't seem to be. And she couldn't kill him while she was landing the plane. She'd be too busy. So he went for it. "So how come you're a complete ghost on social media even though your background check indicates no reason for you to be hiding from anyone?"

It was as though a sudden ice age hit the cockpit. Jasmine froze, her gaze locked on something out the plane's front window, her knuckles turning white as she gripped the yoke. Even her mouth tightened, deep lines etching canyons in her pale face. "Maybe I don't want my business out on the internet for everyone to see. And you had no right to check into my background. *None.* I'm not a criminal. I'm not—"

"I had every right." He kept his voice level, a stark contrast to the fear and anger icing hers. "My intel said you were ferrying opioids and you were armed. It's the business of the Alaska State Troopers to know what they're getting into ahead of time. For all I knew, you were a hired killer with sixteen notches on her belt."

At his words, her face grew even paler. It seemed she had trouble swallowing. For the first time, Will felt a shudder of concern run down his spine. Until this point, she'd been mildly frightened and slightly annoyed. Part of his training was knowing how to read people. And at the mention of assassins, her change in demeanor had tripped all sorts of alarms.

Then her hands started to shake, and Will regretted questioning her while they were airborne. Either she was innocent and frightened enough to freak out and crash this plane or...

Or he'd hit a little too close to home, and Jasmine Jefferson was a cold-blooded killer.

THREE

Fear shot through Jasmine with a painful jolt. Trooper Stryker was too close to the truth, throwing her fragile security into complete and utter chaos.

His questions, his *interference*, could cost her everything if he figured out that her past was not what it said on paper.

Worse, if he saw through her, who else could?

She fought to steady her thoughts and her hands. Thankfully, the landing wasn't off-airport, which would require a lot more focus. While the small dirt strip at Landsher was not as well maintained as the one at Nemeti, the graded runway was better than trying to land in an open field the way she'd have to at their final stop at Loifort.

They bounced to a stop, her entire body trembling so much she could hardly run through shutdown.

As soon as she killed the engine and the airstrip's owner, Harley Bahe, chocked the wheels, Jasmine reached across Will and shoved his door open. "Get off my plane. Now." She straightened and gripped her hands in her lap, praying he couldn't see the tremors in her fingers or hear the shaking in her voice.

He turned toward her, barely banked fire in his eyes. "Ms. Jefferson, I don't think—"

"Now." She shook her head once as Harley watched through the front window, seeming to ask if she was okay. She wasn't, but she couldn't risk him boarding her plane at the moment. She had a text message to send as soon as she was alone. There was no way she'd get off the plane before she sent it either. "Take Scout and get out. Someone can chopper in and get you back to Fairbanks. I'm done."

Will seemed to hold his breath, but then he reached behind him, unhooked Scout and climbed out. When he motioned for the dog to follow, Scout jumped up on the seat and into Will's waiting arms. The pair walked away, leaving the door open.

Jasmine didn't care what he thought of her. She wasn't sure it was worth caring about anything anymore. Because if this thing was as bad as she feared it might be, she could end this day with nothing left to care about anyway. Jerking her personal satellite phone from her hip pocket, she fired off a quick text to a number she'd been forced to memorize two years earlier. State trooper ran my background. He's suspicious. Asking questions. Had a partner with him but not now.

The return text from her WITSEC handler, Deputy Marshal Sam Maldonado, was nearly instantaneous. Why a background search?

False tip that I'm running drugs. Am I safe?

Probably. And anyone who knows your story knows that tip is false.

Should you clear me before this does something to wreck me?

This time, it took longer for the response. Will call the state. Want to know for certain he's legit.

Jasmine froze. It had never crossed her mind that Trooper Stryker might be lying about his identity. What if he'd been sent to kill her and she'd trusted a badge and uniform he'd ordered online?

But the dog...

At the edge of the airstrip, Scout sat at attention beside Will, ready for action. It seemed like a really elaborate con if an assassin had gone to the trouble of training a dog just to take her out of commission.

No. She was just being paranoid. He had a partner and paperwork to prove he was on the up and up. The man *had* to be a legitimate trooper.

Her stomach in knots and her heart racing, Jasmine climbed into the back of the plane, shoved open the cargo door and started passing boxes out to Harley. He paused close to the plane and slid his hat back to scratch his gray hair. The wrinkles on his sun-lined face were etched deeper than usual. "Everything okay?" He kept his voice low, likely to keep Trooper Stryker from hearing from his position about twenty feet away.

"Fine. He's just along for the ride." As much as she'd love to spill about her day to the man who oversaw the small airstrip, she had no desire to blow the trooper's mission, not if he was trying to keep it secret. Jasmine wanted the drug flow to stop as much as he did and, although she didn't trust him, she certainly didn't want to jeopardize his work. "Guess it's been a while since any law enforcement has been this way, and he saw the need to make a patrol. I picked him up in Nemeti."

When she moved to pass a huge bag of rice out to Harley, he laid a hand on hers and looked into her eyes from his position on the ground. "It's a good thing you're doing, letting him fly in with you. It's time someone came out here to check on us. They flew Casey Bell out in a helicopter two days ago. Overdose."

Jasmine's shoulders slumped. Casey Bell ran a small wildlife rehab center ten miles from the airstrip and often helped Harley keep the makeshift runway graded. "What did he take?"

"I haven't heard. I just know it wasn't good when he left." With a quick pat of her hand, he went back to his job, stacking the cargo onto the back of an ancient four-wheeler so he could haul it to the locked storage shed. People from outlying areas would come in and get their shipments as they were able.

Jasmine sat back on her heels and watched him drive away. He nodded his head at the trooper as he passed, and the trooper looked up from his satellite phone long enough to nod back.

Harley was right. Someone needed to check up on the people she cared about, the people she served. And no one knew the flight paths better than she did. What if she offered a truce to Trooper Stryker? Allowed him to tag along with her for more than one day while he figured out who the real bad guys were? It would be uncomfortable, but her discomfort would be a small price to pay to put a choke hold on the drug trade on the frontier.

When her sat phone buzzed in her pocket, she glanced at the number and pulled it to her ear, her heart picking up speed. She glanced at the small storage pouch by her seat where she stored her pistol. If that man wasn't a real law enforcement officer after all…

Pulling in a deep breath, she answered the phone.

"Jasmine." Deputy Marshal Maldonado's voice was professional yet friendly. "Are you safe?"

"I am. I hope. You tell me."

"Trooper Will Stryker is legit. I spoke to his colonel. If you're looking at a tall, dark-haired, dark-eyed trooper with a border collie named Scout as a partner, then you're looking at Will Stryker."

Across the space between them, he seemed to sense they were talking about him and glanced up. "I am."

"Good. Your identity is safe. I did a cursory check and it doesn't appear anyone has accessed your witness protection file. No one is coming after you today."

"You're sure?" Trusting was difficult, but the deputy had never steered her wrong.

"You can fly Trooper Stryker wherever he needs to go…and he will leave you this evening none the wiser. The only way this would become an issue is if he was joining you long-term. We'd have to find a way to answer his questions then." Maldonado cleared his throat. "His colonel informed me he's pretty relentless when he smells trouble. And while it's not unusual to let law enforcement know your situation, I'd advise against letting too many people find out."

"So, what happens if he flies with me for longer than today?" The words were out before she could stop them. The implosion of her life two years ago had started because she wanted to help. She'd fled her life in Los Angeles after witnessing a drug hit gone wrong. Testifying had cost Jasmine her name, her second-grade classroom and her family. While her life had gone up in flames and she'd been looking over her shoulder ever since, taking the stand had been worth it. Her testimony had put contract killer Anton Rogers into maximum security prison for life.

He'd vowed revenge. A bomb beneath her car shortly after he was locked away said that he could still reach her, even from prison. When he targeted her for execution, Yasmine Carlisle had died so that Jasmine Jefferson could be born.

"What do you mean by him flying with you for more than just today?" Deputy Maldonado shifted from skeptical to resigned. "You want to help him, don't you?"

Jasmine said nothing. She didn't have to. The deputy marshal knew her well. Even if she found herself in danger again, she couldn't turn her back on the people of Alaska.

Maldonado exhaled loudly. It was hard to tell if he was frustrated or simply resigned to the fact that God had given her a personality that couldn't help but serve others. "I can't tell you not to, but you have to understand that if you want to work with him and alleviate all of his suspicions about you, then you'll likely have to allow me to tell him the truth about who you are. And that means, when this is over, it broadens the possibility that you could have to leave Alaska in order to guarantee your safety."

No. Alaska was her home now. It had taken two years, but she finally felt safe here. Felt like she was doing the work God had created her to do. Her job was crucial to people's survival. She was good at it, and she got to fly, which was the thing she loved most in the world. In fact, it was one of the things she'd refused to give up when she moved into protection.

But if it meant saving lives by slicing the head off the dragon…

Jasmine turned away from Will and stared across the undulating land to the mountains in the distance. With a sigh, she surrendered the life she loved. "Tell him."

Head tilted toward his phone, Will surreptitiously watched Jasmine as she disconnected her call and stared at the device. She'd initially appeared disturbed but, based on her straightened posture, she'd apparently come to some sort of resolve.

That resolve had better not involve leaving him at this remote outpost. Or dumping his body somewhere nearby.

Now she sat in the cargo door, legs dangling over the side of the plane. She observed him as though waiting for something. For him to apologize again? Maybe—

His phone vibrated and indicated a blocked number. Interesting. He flicked the screen and answered. "Stryker."

"Trooper Will Stryker?" The man's voice was brusque. All business.

Will's pulse picked up. "Yes."

"I'm Deputy US Marshal Sam Maldonado."

His eyes narrowed, and he watched Jasmine jump from the plane. Her lower lip was drawn between her teeth. Gone was the tough woman who'd booted him off her plane. Clearly, this call had everything to do with her. "Go ahead."

"We need to talk about Jasmine Jefferson."

He knew it. She was on the run. He wasn't fond of arresting her out here alone, but if—

"Trooper, I'm with Witness Security."

The phone nearly slipped through Will's fingers. Of all the things he'd expected, that wasn't one of them. "WITSEC?" He scrubbed his hand along the back of his neck. What sort of trouble had he unleashed for Jasmine by checking into her background?

Beside him, Scout stood and pressed his nose to Will's calf, sensing the tension.

"I'll forward proof to you and your colonel over secure channels, but you can trust her. She wants to help you." The voice lost some of its businesslike tone. "Even if it means giving up her life a second time. She can tell you more, but know she will put herself in danger to protect others."

"I can see that. What did she do to merit protection?" He was fishing. Was she a bad actor who'd turned on someone else to save herself?

"She's an innocent civilian who chose to give up her life to put away a criminal. Be careful with what she's giving you." The deputy marshal ended the call.

By the time Will gathered his thoughts, Jasmine had completed her preflight and climbed into her seat where she sat waiting. He hefted Scout into the plane, secured him and took his seat. "Is there anything you want to talk about?"

She lifted the headset. "Not over these." She held up a hand to stop Harley as he walked out to remove the wheel chocks. When he backed away with a puzzled expression, she spoke. "I'll tell you the short version, but we don't discuss it in flight over headsets."

Understandable. Even though the odds were against

someone overhearing a cockpit transmission, it could still happen.

"I was a teacher in California. I was out running errands in a neighborhood I'd never visited before." She fiddled with her seat belt. "I saw a man in an alley shoot another man in the back of the head. And he saw me. I made it to a police station before he caught up."

Her voice was emotionless. She was clearly leaving out the details, holding the horrors of that day at bay.

Will nearly reached over and took her hand, then he remembered who he was and what his job was and opted for professionalism.

"It wasn't a simple murder. He was a hired killer responsible for dozens of deaths, and he was contracted to an upstart cartel run by Dasha Melnyk. My testimony put Anton in jail, and he cut a deal." She released a quavering breath. "His testimony shut down the cartel's operations entirely. When he threatened me, and one of his signature bombs showed up under my car after the trial, I wound up here. He proved he could reach me from the inside."

Dasha Melnyk. He knew a little about the case. The cartel had crumbled, and Melnyk had disappeared somewhere in Romania, rumored dead at the hands of her biggest rival.

Jasmine finally faced him, eyes wide with fear—or determination. Will wasn't quite sure which.

"I've been flying since I was sixteen, although it was a hobby. It was the one part of my life WITSEC let me keep. I love Alaska. Love supplying people who'd be cut off and in danger without us." She swept her hand across the cockpit toward the wide-open spaces before them. "I don't want to jeopardize this life, but if it will stop drug runners from destroying more lives, I'll do whatever it takes." Without waiting for him to comment, she slipped on her headset and motioned for Harley to remove the wheel chocks before she started the plane. "If Jesus can die for me, then…"

Will slid on his headset but remained silent. She would lay her life down for people she hardly knew and most of whom she'd never meet. But she loved them enough to give up everything, and her words echoed ones he knew all too well, words he tried to live by. "You're a Christian?"

As the plane coasted to a stop before takeoff, she nodded. Before he could say more, they'd bumped down the runway and were airborne, headed to Loifort, a little less than an hour's flight away. He'd already been warned it was a remote location with no grounds crew or staff, but flying in would give him the lay of the land.

Every day, Will recited Christ's words in his head, prepared to literally die for the people of Alaska. But he'd never considered that dying might also mean continuing to breathe while giving up everything to survive.

"Why do you do what you do, Trooper?" Jasmine's voice crackled in his ear, but she kept her eyes on the gauges and the sky before them. "You don't seem like the type to enjoy running around the wilds of Alaska."

"Oh?" Will angled his body toward her, willing to engage in conversation. She ran deeper than he'd anticipated, had flipped sideways everything he'd assumed about her. Had reminded him of what fellow trooper Helena Maddox said way too often. *It's innocent until proven guilty, Stryker. Not the other way around. Your unwillingness to remember that is going to get you into trouble one day.*

It nearly had today. "So what type of guy do I seem like?"

She nearly smiled. It was a first, and he had to admit it was attractive. "You're all spit and polish, kind of like if your uniform got mud on it, you'd freak out. I'm guessing there's stain remover in your backpack."

He laughed and, when he did, the air in the plane seemed to lighten. "Nope. The spit and polish is part of the job. I hate shining and ironing. You should have seen me a few weeks ago, crawling in the mud trying to locate a poacher. I loved every minute of it."

"Hard to imagine you muddy, Trooper."

"Call me Will." He held out his hand, realizing he'd never actually introduced himself.

She gave his hand a quick shake, and this time she really did smile, lighting up the full force of a grin. "Wait. Will Stryker? Did your parents have a random name generator for cops? That sounds like a purposely heroic name." She dropped her chin and her voice. "Will Stryker. Defender of the innocent."

He chuckled. It wasn't the first time he'd been poked about the name. "I had it legally changed. It was originally Humbert Hubert."

"That's not true." With her secret in the open, something had changed. It sure was making this flight more comfortable than their previous one.

"You're right, but it makes a good story."

This time when she smiled, the man in Will noticed. From behind his sunglasses, he watched as she guided the plane through the air, navigating shifting air currents along the edge of the mountains. She was confident and capable, at ease in the cockpit in a way he envied. With her chin-length hair waving darkly from beneath the ball cap she'd smashed over it, he had to admit she was a beautiful woman.

Something he shouldn't be noticing. He watched the wilderness below roll away to mountains, crisscrossed with waterways. All of this would be frozen soon, an entirely different sort of dangerous wonderland.

There was a long, companionable silence, one he was reluctant to break. Finally, the splendor around him drove Will to speak. "I'll never get used to the wild out here. Or to the way it stays daylight until after midnight."

"That took some getting used to. I've been here two years and I'm just now getting to where I can sleep." She adjusted her grip on the yoke. "Are you really from Kansas, or did you just say that to get a reaction from me?"

He nodded, acknowledging that she'd caught him. "Minnesota. When they started the K-9 unit here, I wanted to be a part of it." That, and Minnesota had too many rough memories. Memories of why he'd gone into law enforcement. Memories of how criminals never played fair.

"You didn't answer my original question." This time, she faced him and, although she wore sunglasses, he couldn't tear away from the directness of her gaze. "Why do you do this? If we're working together, I'd like to know your level of commitment." Gone were the smile and the teasing tone. She was laying her life on the line for him and for the people she served.

He could at least tell her the truth he held close to his bulletproof vest.

Will tapped the side of his headset to remind her

someone might be listening. He wasn't interested in broadcasting his entire story to the world. "The short version is that my mother..." Emotion rushed his chest in a way that it hadn't in a long time. Something about the small cockpit and the hum of the engines made the telling more difficult. He pulled in a deep breath and opted for the easy way out. "My mother was an addict." That was all she needed to know.

Only Jasmine's sigh broke the hum of static in his headset, and then her hand was on his. She gave his fingers a quick squeeze before she withdrew, almost as though she'd never touched him.

But the warmth lingered. It crept up his arm and into his chest, loosening the bands there, making him want to say more. To tell her how it had felt when his mother had overdosed—not by accident and not by suicide. How it had felt when, at eighteen, he'd had to identify her at the morgue. How he'd dropped out of college and done four years in the army before he'd found himself and decided to go into law enforcement. How his job had led to yet another thrashing of his heart. Things he'd never—

"We have a problem." Jasmine's voice cut into his chaotic thoughts. When he turned, she was staring at a gauge in front of her, then she leaned over to look at the one in front of him.

For the first time, he realized the engines sounded different, as though they might be struggling.

"The gauges don't back me up, but..." Jasmine looked straight at him, her mouth a grim line. "I'm pretty sure we're out of fuel."

"Whoa. *What?*" Every muscle in Will's body tightened. While he wasn't afraid of flying, crashing was a whole other story.

"We had fuel when I checked. Gauges say we do. But the engines—" A sputtering cough cut through her words. "Both engines aren't getting fuel." She switched on the radio. "Mayday, mayday, mayday. This is Nevada five-seven-five-xray-romeo." She repeated the information and gave their situation and location.

The radio remained silent.

Jasmine repeated the call, again with no answer. With a frustrated huff, she flipped switches and adjusted half a dozen things he had no idea what to call. "We should be getting a response on the radio. It's dead."

Will balled his fists, working hard not to focus on the eerie silence. A dead radio and no fuel? He didn't believe in that much coincidence. "Now what?"

"Now we land it like a glider." She glanced sideways at him. "It can be done, but it's rough. And my best option is right there." She pulled her hand from the yoke only long enough to indicate a flat open area between a river and a mountain. "We're fine as long as we don't get a downdraft or lose altitude too fast. Make sure you and Scout are secured."

Scout. Will reached behind him and laid his hand on his partner's head. He'd never felt so out of control. There was nothing he could do but watch and trust.

And pray.

The quiet after the engine sounds was loud, but he didn't dare speak as Jasmine made adjustments and gripped the yoke so tightly her knuckles were white.

The ground grew closer.

"Get ready." Jasmine muttered the words, her concentration clearly on her job.

Should he brace for impact? Fireballs and flipping planes raced across his mind, but he forced them aside and prayed without actual words. They'd be safe. They had to be.

The plane hit hard, bounced, hit again then immediately seemed to slide left toward the mountain. Why wasn't she steering away? "What are you doing?"

"Tire blew." She fought the plane for control as the mountain loomed larger. "Will. Pray."

FOUR

The plane fought her best efforts to turn it away from the slope at the bottom of the mountain. They couldn't hit it. At best, the slope would tear off a wing. At worst?

She couldn't think of the worst.

Finally, the plane bounced and slowed, coming to a stop perpendicular to her intended landing area, facing the frontier that stretched out toward the river.

Jasmine exhaled the breath she'd been holding, slumped in her seat and forced tight muscles to relax. She flexed her fingers, not entirely certain she wasn't dead.

Beside her, Will sank back into his seat as well. "What happened?"

"A blown tire makes it a battle to control the plane on the ground." Without power, she'd glided into the uneven ground and likely hit something that took out the tire and threw off her ability to steer.

"That was some amazing piloting." His voice was all admiration and relief.

"That was a lot of prayer." Jasmine pulled off her headset, released her seat belt and leaned forward, trying to catch her breath as reality kicked in. The plane could have flipped. She fired a very sincere prayer to her God that it hadn't.

Still, this day couldn't get much worse. She'd had weapons aimed at her. Had nearly been arrested. Was hauling around a man who was at times amiable and at times combative.

Now, the beloved Twin Otter, her favorite plane in the Kesuk Aviation fleet, had betrayed her in multiple ways. She didn't want to think about how that could have happened. She glanced sideways at Will. Something about the way the trooper was focused on his knees drew her attention to him. "You're not a fan of flying, are you?"

He seemed to come back from a distance. "In the army, I jumped out of planes frequently. Enjoyed the ride down under canopy more than the ride up in the plane." He arched an eyebrow. "However, I am definitely not a fan of what just happened, and I'm already sitting here praying I never repeat the experience." Now that he'd spoken, some of the tension seemed to leave him. He reached back and scratched Scout's ears.

The collie seemed none the worse for wear and closed his eyes in bliss at the attention.

If he could be calm, so could she. After all, she was the pilot and she'd gotten them down safely. The danger was behind them. She could fall apart over their near miss when she was home behind closed doors. "Well, thankfully we're safe. But I have to call back and let my company know what's going on. I'm going to need a mechanic ASAP if we're going to get out of here before nightfall." That was still a lot of hours away, but she didn't want to push it.

Jasmine unbuckled her seat belt and shoved open her

door. "I'll see if I can't figure out why the gauges aren't working." And why she was out of fuel in the first place. She'd flown this route dozens of times. Never once had she come even remotely close to running on fumes.

As for the sudden loss of the radio? It had been working when she checked it before takeoff. The malfunction had to be a coincidence. Anything else was too terrifying to consider.

Will was suddenly in motion. "Is there anything I can do?"

"Not at the moment. I'll let you know." She grabbed the satellite phone and climbed out of the plane. Relief sank into her, almost weakening her knees as she walked toward the nearby river. While she was used to being solo out on the frontier, she wouldn't deny Will's company was welcome if she was stranded for a few hours.

She dialed the office and the phone rang three times before Darrin Hawkins, one of the owners, picked up. "Jasmine? Everything okay?"

"Why wouldn't it be?" Darrin wasn't one to panic easily, but his voice held an edge.

"You don't usually call on the sat phone. And…" He trailed off like a guilty preschooler caught with his hand in the candy jar.

"And you could have warned me I was going to be boarded by the state troopers today." She watched Will heft Scout down from the plane. "A heads-up would have been nice. They scared me to death."

"Actually, I couldn't. A team showed up here and wanted permission to board the plane. They told me there was a tip, but I wasn't allowed to contact you. They were afraid you'd divert or drop cargo, I guess."

Jasmine sighed. Darrin was right. If she was a bad guy, that was exactly what she'd have done.

"So what's going on now? By my calculations, you should be at Loifort. Is everything okay?"

"Not exactly." She relayed the fuel issue to him, as well as the trouble with the gauges and the radio. "And to boot, I've got a passenger. You should have my location on the locator beacon. Can you send Jerry up with some fuel and his toolbox? Oh, and a let him know we blew a tire." Jerry was an ace mechanic. He'd have the plane squared away and in the air in no time.

"You have a *passenger*?" There was a rustle and some clicks of a mouse. "That's not on my manifest."

"It's the state trooper who boarded. He's hopping a ride back to Fairbanks with me." That was enough said. She could fill Darrin in on the details later. Right now, all she wanted to hear was that Jerry was on the way and that they could get out of here before darkness set in at 10:30. That was still half a day away, but given the hour it would take Jerry to get to them and the time it would take him to repair the airplane, she didn't want to be flying back in the dark.

"You should have let us know you'd picked up a passenger."

"Been a lot going on today, Darrin. Now, how soon can you get Jerry out here? I can do a minimal amount of checking to see what's wrong, but I can't repair the plane."

"Jerry flew to Anchorage to pick up a part for the Cessna."

"What about Keith?"

"He flew out today in the King Air and won't be back for a couple of hours, and Manny's out recovering from surgery. I'll call Jerry back in, but it's going to take him at least an hour to get here once they get to the airport and take off, then he'll have to load up and get to you. You may be camping tonight, Jas."

She wanted to sink to the ground at the thought. She'd been looking forward to a hot bath and an early bedtime. The idea of sleeping on the floor of the plane after the day she'd already had was almost too much. "You're sure?"

"You have emergency gear, your pistol and an Alaska State Trooper to keep you safe. You'll be fine."

She scowled. "You think I can't take care of myself?" Sometimes, she really hated being a woman in a man's world. "I'm not afraid of being out here alone. I just wanted hot food tonight."

"That's not what I meant and you know it." Darrin chuckled. "Build a campfire and do some hunting. Hot food in no time."

"Bye, Darrin." Killing the call, she walked to the Twin Otter to lean her head against the plane's metal skin. Jasmine wasn't afraid to stay in the bush. She'd camped alone before, but never by necessity. If she were being honest, she was ready to drop Will off and be alone. To process this day and spend some time with Jesus.

Not camp out in the wilds with the man who messed with her head and her emotions.

"Everything okay?" Will's voice reached her at the same time Scout did.

The dog nudged her calf with his nose, looking up with soulful brown eyes.

Somehow, the dog seemed to get it. Jasmine crouched and cupped his adorable face in her hands, then scratched behind both of his ears before she glanced up at Will. "Hope you like camping. Looks like you might get a shot at seeing the aurora after all, though not from the air."

"No help until tomorrow?"

"Probably not." She stood and brushed off her knees. "We're fairly safe out here. We can bunk in the plane and there's an emergency kit with food and gear. Biggest danger is bear, but they can't breach the plane."

Will pulled out his sat phone. "I have to call in. Where's the nearest village?"

"Couple of hours by four-wheeler. There are some remote settlers out here, but even they're a good distance away so I doubt we'll see them. Even if someone happened by, they won't be able to do much for us."

"I just need a location."

"I can give you the lat and long, if you want a helicopter to pick you up." She couldn't leave. The plane was hers to protect, but there was nothing to keep him here.

"I'm not leaving you alone. I'm fine rocking the wilderness life." Will grinned and walked away, Scout close at his heels.

Jasmine leaned against the plane and crossed her arms, watching the trooper reach down to pet the collie as he spoke into the phone. His deep voice drifted back to her, though she couldn't make out the words.

Something about him drew her, but that made no sense. Could be because he knew her secret and she was free to talk openly for the first time in two years, something she hadn't realized she longed to do until now.

It didn't matter. Her life wasn't her own, and it never would be. When Will moved to his next case, there was a possibility she could move, too. Forced into a new life, one that prevented her from touching an airplane again.

Deep inside, where her soul connected with her God, she knew this was what she was meant to do. Flying planes, helping others… It was a solid truth in her life, a calling she'd never questioned. How could it be that in helping Will, she could possibly lose that calling?

At the moment, however, they had more pressing problems. The least she could do was peek at the engine and electronics. While her knowledge involved a basic working understanding of the parts "under the hood," she could provide Jerry with a starting spot before he arrived.

She hauled out the ladder and popped the hatch over the engine. Immediately the smell of fuel overwhelmed everything else. Jasmine leaned away to let it dissipate, then eased closer. That was definitely *not* right. Her eyes trailed the fuel line and stopped at a gash in the hose. A straight, clean gash that hadn't happened naturally and that had caused a fuel leak that should have registered in her gauges.

Jasmine gripped the ladder, her palms growing clammy.

"What's wrong?" Will's voice came from below.

She didn't turn from the plane. This wasn't happening. It *couldn't* be.

"Jasmine?"

Pulling in a deep breath, she gripped the ladder. It didn't matter if she helped Will or not. She was already in danger. And she was staring at the proof. "Someone tried to kill us."

Will punched the rolled jacket under his head and wished for the hundredth time it was his pillow on his bed. Beside him, Scout tucked closer, his back pressed against the sleeping bag over Will's stomach.

At least one of them was getting some rest tonight.

After a dinner of emergency rations from a stash in the plane, Jasmine had produced two sleeping bags and had unrolled hers near the rear of the cargo area while he tried to bed down near the front.

Sleep had proven elusive, though. For one thing, it had taken until almost eleven for the sky to grow dark. For a guy who slept with blackout curtains, that had made things tough enough.

But Jasmine's insistence that the plane had been tampered with added a whole new level to this insomnia. If she was right, then was she the target? Or was he…? And when had the plane been hit? Things could have gone south before she even left Fairbanks. Or, after he'd accepted the invitation to fly with her, someone could have targeted him at either of the two airfields where the plane spent time on the ground.

Will exhaled loudly. It would be nice to roll over to his other side, but he really didn't want to wake Scout. The dog needed sleep as much as he did.

"Are you still awake, too?" From the back of the plane, Jasmine's whisper drifted forward as though she didn't want to disturb him.

"Am I keeping you up?" All of his restlessness and worry had likely reached her ears. "Sorry."

"It's not you. My backpack makes a terrible pillow. Couldn't sleep, so I've been praying about Casey Bell's overdose. About catching the traffickers. About a lot of things."

She said it so easily. Will hadn't even considered praying his sleepless night through. His Bible time was at six every morning, like clockwork. An appointment with God that he never missed.

There was a rustle in the darkness and the plane rocked slightly. "You were talking about the aurora earlier. Since we're both awake, we could open the door and see what's out there. I can't see out the front windows from here, but it seems like the light is shifting." This time, her voice was closer, somewhere near the middle of the plane where the cargo door was firmly closed against the night creatures that roamed the frontier.

He sat up quickly, and Scout was just as fast, rising before Will even reached the zipper for the sleeping bag. He'd been fascinated by the northern lights since his move to Alaska. Seeing them out here on the frontier was a long-held dream. While he'd been in the wilderness many times, those visits had never coincided with a night when the aurora was active. "Think there will be a show tonight?"

The plane rocked again, then the door slid open. "I think you're blessed to see this season's premier." Jasmine's silhouette darkened the doorway.

Beyond her lay a whole other world.

Will scrambled out of the sleeping bag with Scout close beside. At the doorway, he settled in next to Jasmine, who sat with her legs dangling over the side. The sky undulated and waved slowly in a green-curtained dance at once otherworldly eerie and God-created beautiful. His heart tugged toward the sight, proof of the creativity of the Creator who knew no limits. Something inside him reacted in a way that reading his Bible each morning had never produced. Something intimate and personal toward his Maker.

"Wild, isn't it?" Jasmine's voice was barely a whisper. Her shoulder brushed his in the narrow door space before she angled slightly away. "That this exists. That the sky can do this incredible thing."

"Yet people still don't believe in God." He kept his voice low, somehow lost in the holy reverence of the moment.

"There's a lot of ugly in the world. So many reasons to be afraid and angry. Then you see this, and you realize it dances on whether we're here or not. We can't change it. Only God can. And somehow—"

"It makes the ugly seem less ugly."

"Mmm-hmm."

They watched in silence. The frontier sat before them in total stillness. The motion of the sky was so vast, it almost seemed as though there should be some noise along with it. Some unearthly music. "It's so quiet."

"The aurora actually has a sound." Jasmine braced her hands by her hips, so close to Will's leg that he could feel the warmth, and leaned forward into the openness around them. "It pops and crackles, but you really have to be listening."

Will mimicked her posture, and their fingers brushed. If he wanted, he could wrap his fingers around hers and—

But why would he do that? He drew back quickly and sat up straighter, resting his hands on his knees. Behind him, Scout snored softly, his back against Will's, oblivious to the beauty before them. "I'll take your word for it."

Jasmine chuckled, unaware of his wayward thoughts, then she grew quiet. "So, you know why I'm here in Alaska. What ugly I'm running from in the world." She nudged his elbow with hers. "What brought *you* here?"

Will stiffened. How did she know he'd been running when he came to this wild land? "What do you mean?"

"You've been here a few years, but this is your first frontier aurora viewing. That seems a little off. From everything you say, your job is your life. Then there's the way you talk, like you didn't come to Alaska to experience Alaska. To live in a land rougher than any other. You came here for another reason. And in my experience?" She eased away from him, leaning against the door frame, though her silhouette said she still watched the beauty before her. "People either come to Alaska because they're drawn to its uniqueness or because they're running from something in the lower forty-eight."

How had she done that? Hit so close to the truth after knowing him only twelve hours? He cleared his throat. "Maybe God called me here."

"The way you got all tight and sat up straighter when I asked the question says something different." She chuckled softly. "I taught second graders, remember? They are the world's worst at hiding their body language. Teachers know how to read their students. Besides, if we're going to work together and you know my truth, shouldn't I know yours?"

Her truth. Will had started this day convinced he'd close it out with the arrest of a hard-core drug smuggler. He'd convicted Jasmine in his heart and mind before his helicopter ever landed at Nemeti.

It was still possible she was guilty, though. Just because her plane had been clean today, that didn't mean it always was. She could simply be a very good con artist.

He knew all about very good con artists.

Still, the tip implicating her had been wrong, and

he wasn't sure what that meant when it came to his job or to God.

Or to Jasmine. Cynicism was a part of his nature, but Jasmine had challenged that today. And she challenged him even more so now as they shared this incredible moment when the sky danced to a tune only God could orchestrate.

Even though it made no sense to his head, his heart wanted to trust her. For the first time in his life, he wanted to talk. To unburden himself to another human being. Maybe because she was a stranger. Or perhaps because the setting was so, well, intimate.

But he'd never even told God these things. How could he confide in Jasmine, who he still wasn't certain was an innocent woman, the darkest secrets of his heart?

FIVE

Pressing her shoulder tighter against the door frame, Jasmine kept her gaze on the shimmering green and purple lights that painted the sky in an unnervingly beautiful, motion-filled work of art.

Inwardly, her stomach seemed to shrink. What was she thinking, asking Trooper Will Stryker such a thing? They weren't friends. They were on brand-new speaking terms after the fiasco of the day. Yet, sitting here, dependent on each other's company to pass the time, she genuinely wanted to know who this man was. She'd confessed her secret—at least in part—and part of her wanted to level the playing field, to restore balance by hearing his as well.

But Will was silent. Tension radiated from him as he pressed his hands against the floor and leaned into the night to see past the plane's door, which opened over their heads like a porch roof. Even in the darkness lit only by the aurora and the stars, it was clear his jaw was clenched. His eyes were fixed on the sky, but Jasmine had to wonder if he saw the ethereal beauty.

There was nothing to do but sit in awkward silence. Her prying had wrecked a peaceful moment they'd both sorely needed. For the first time since she'd looked at her engine, she'd forgotten the plane had likely been tampered with. Had forgotten her life in Alaska might be cut short. Had forgotten—

"Minnesota and Alaska are both cold." Will's words stalled her thoughts. It seemed the words came from deep inside him, pulled to the surface slowly and laboriously. "When I was twelve, my mom was involved in an accident at work. She got hooked on Oxy. It happened fast. Really fast. Me being a kid, I didn't notice. Maybe if I had…" He shrugged. "Maybe it would have been different."

"You were twelve. No kid is going to see those kinds of signs or, if they do, know what to do about them."

"Maybe. I mean, looking back now that I'm thirty, it all makes sense. But I wish I'd seen it then."

The urge to reach for him nearly swamped Jasmine. The teacher in her wanted to comfort that twelve-year-old and to tell him it would all be okay. But this was no middle schooler. This was a man wrestling with a past he was still trying to make sense of. There was little she could—or should—do about that.

Except listen.

"Naturally, she burned her bridges with all of the doctors and the pharmacies, so she went the illegal route. At some point, she got in over her head with her dealer, so she started selling for him. I'm not clear on the timeline, but when I was about fifteen or sixteen, she almost seemed less tense for a while." He shook his head and leaned back, stretching his arms and shoulders before he sat forward again. "It was a weird combo of less stressed but more anxious. Maybe because she had a steady supply of drugs but knew what she was doing was wrong. I'm sure watching her back for the police every day wore on her. And worrying what would happen to me probably did, too. Eventually, she tried to turn on her dealer. She went to the cops and offered to turn him over." Will shook his head and looked Jasmine in the eye. "She was trying to get clean and to make everything right."

His voice was the same level it had always been, but a raw anguish made the edges jagged. She probably would have missed it in any other situation, but the silence of the night magnified the sound of his pain. She couldn't help but reach out to him.

Her hand found his and held on, trying to give him some comfort, praying for his pain to be healed by the only One who could.

Will started to pull away, but then he curled his fingers around hers and looked into the night again. "It was two months after I left for college. She waited until I was out of the house to make her move against the guy. Figured it was safer for me, I guess. Later, when I became a cop and could get into the records, I found out exactly what happened, but I didn't know for years." His grip tightened. "The detectives wired her and sent her in to pick up a stash to sell, but Mom was always a terrible liar." He laughed, sharp and bitter. "They figured her out, and murdered her. You can kill an average man with pure fentanyl equal to four grains of salt, but they shot her up with enough to kill thirty men twice her size. The dealers were angry she turned on them, and they made an example out of her."

Emotion almost closed Jasmine's throat, but she held it in. He needed her to carry his pain, not to express it in a way that would force him to comfort her.

"They caught a couple of the lower-level guys in the operation, but their leader evaded arrest. He died about five years ago in a power grab. He was drowned in his bathtub."

Jasmine's eyes drifted closed. The man whose murder she'd witnessed had been killed because he crossed a drug cartel. Will's story intersected with hers in a way that lacerated her system. They were mirrors reflecting two sides of evil. "That's why you came to Alaska." It made sense. They'd both had a drive for justice, and it had changed the course of both of their lives.

"No. That's why I became a cop." He pulled his hand from hers and stretched his arms out in front of him, fingers laced together. Then he pressed his back against the door frame, one leg dangling into space and the other bent, his knee barely brushing her thigh.

She tried to ignore the contact. After holding his hand, his touch evoked more emotion than it should. She cleared her throat to sweep it away. "So…Alaska?"

He laughed, but it didn't sound as though it was born out of humor. More out of bitterness. "Alaska was because of a woman."

"Ah." Jasmine mimicked his posture. Their knees touched in the narrow space. Maybe this would make the mood lighter. "You followed her here?"

"I ran from her here." He tipped his head back and rested it against the plane. "You really want to hear my life story?"

"Neither of us is sleeping. And it's preferable to wondering who sabotaged my plane. Or if it was really sabotaged at all." Because maybe she was so paranoid that she was imagining things. But too many things had happened at once and that cut was too perfect for it all to be accidental.

"I get your point." This time, when he chuckled, it sounded like he was genuinely amused. "So my past gets sacrificed for your present comfort?"

"Something like that."

"Okay, but you're going to owe me more stories about Jasmine Jefferson. I want embarrassing stuff. Like how you tripped in front of your high school crush. Something ridiculously lighthearted."

"Your definition of lighthearted is kind of mean." Jasmine smiled anyway. She understood what he was going for. Distraction, the same as she was. "And my real name is…" No. It was too much to tell him now. "Let's just say she would be the one with the embarrassing high school stories." Because *Yasmine* wasn't Jasmine Jefferson. *She* was a different person who no longer existed, even though she still lived in Jasmine.

The thought always brought a shudder. How could someone be dead and yet still live?

Seeming to sense her discomfort, Will pressed his knee against hers briefly and changed the subject. "I really did come to Alaska because of the K-9 unit, but I was looking for a way out of Minnesota. It does something to a guy when he finds out that his girlfriend, the one he was certain he was going to marry, is only using him for protection."

"Protection?" Because she was afraid of the world and thought being married to a cop would keep her safe?

"She was a midlevel dealer. Heroin. Beth never used the stuff herself so I never saw the signs. She thought having me in her pocket would protect her if she ever got caught."

"Will, no. That's awful." The words poured out in a gasp. That explained his readiness to believe Jasmine was guilty before he even met her.

"When she finally got arrested, she found out real fast that I wouldn't turn my back on the badge for her." His voice grew tight and somber. "It's embarrassing, really. I can't believe I told you."

She couldn't believe it either. It was such a painful, personal story. His life was full of so much that she couldn't even fathom. There had to be something she could say, something she could *give* him, to ease some of the hurt. "I'm sorry about what your girlfriend did. You're too good of a person to have been treated that way, and I hope someday you realize that."

Will froze and, when he spoke, his voice was ice. "I hope I never forget what she did." He crossed his arms over his chest. "I'm never getting betrayed like that again. I'm fine the way I am. Keeps me focused on the job."

The blunt words rolled in her stomach like rough turbulence. Trooper Will Stryker was a man with high walls, ones no one but God could ever break down. She'd be praying that—

A low growl rolled between them, and Scout stood, staring into the night.

Will's gaze followed the border collie's, and he watched the darkness intently.

"What's wrong?" Jasmine's radar started to ping. They'd seen something. Something neither of them liked.

But he merely shook his head. "Nothing. Probably an animal. I'm going to go take a look around just to be sure." He looked at Scout and pointed to Jasmine. "Stay. Guard."

Without waiting for an answer from Jasmine, he jumped down from the plane. "Close the door. Get some sleep. I'll be back in a little while."

She wanted to argue, to ask where he was going, but something in his tone told her she'd better do as he said. That same gut feeling also said he wasn't telling her the whole truth.

Closing the door, Jasmine crept back to her sleeping bag and sat with her back against the wall.

A few feet away, Scout sat with his back to her, watching the door.

She wrapped her arms around her knees, closed her eyes and prayed.

As soon as Jasmine secured the door, Will drew his pistol, confident Scout would alert him should anyone try to get into the plane. Jasmine was in good hands with the best partner in the world.

Sure, he hadn't told her the whole truth, but there was no need to frighten her unnecessarily when she was already on edge. Likely whatever Scout had scented and alerted to was a bear or a moose, but he couldn't take that chance. The possibility that her plane had been tampered with meant someone might have set the entire thing up to leave them vulnerable to attack on the open frontier.

And it was likely because of him. He'd boarded her plane at Nemeti and was with her at Landsher. It was a high probability the bad guys knew he was looking for them and would do whatever it took to shut him down. He should have seen this coming.

But he'd been so certain Jasmine was guilty that he hadn't thought past taking her into custody. He dragged his hand down his face. His teammate Helena Maddox was right. It was possible his overly suspicious nature had landed him, his partner and Jasmine in deep trouble.

Will wiped a bead of sweat off his temple, hating himself for it. He'd been a police officer for years and had had his share of time on the Alaskan frontier but tonight, even with the northern lights dancing overhead, this felt a whole lot like his time in Afghanistan. The mountain before him, unseen assailants around him… Some memories were best left in the past.

He scanned the side of the mountain then surveyed the flat land from the plane to the horizon as the lights in the sky shifted the shadows on the ground. While beautiful, the depth of the lights on the frontier, where the world was deathly silent, lent an unearthly feeling to the darkness, as though he watched from inside a twisted nightmare.

Nothing moved. If Scout hadn't alerted, Will would think he'd dreamed the whole thing.

Holstering his sidearm, he scrubbed his face with both hands. No doubt he was exhausted, but sleep wasn't coming anytime soon. Might as well patrol the area. Maybe if he convinced himself all was well, his mind would shut down and let him rest.

Keeping his hand on the grip of his holstered sidearm, he made a slow circuit around the plane, then eyed the flat frontier once again. There was still no motion.

Which, come to think of it, was kind of strange. Shouldn't there be night creatures roaming around?

Maybe their presence and the hulk of the plane was keeping them at bay, but still...it seemed odd.

It also made the hair on the back of his neck stand at attention. At least overseas or when he was in the field with his team, there were other sets of eyes and more people to see what he couldn't. Right now, it was only him. And he was very capable of missing something.

Feeling as though a thousand eyes watched him, Will walked toward the slope of the mountain away from the plane, wishing he'd grabbed his flashlight, but he clearly wasn't thinking straight. Jasmine had gotten to him earlier. Had him talking about things he never talked about. It had to have been the aurora and the moment. He was done with relationships. He sure wasn't feeling things for a woman who, just over twelve hours ago, had been his prime suspect.

And he needed to get his head back into the game, before he missed something that got one or both of them hurt.

A soft rustle to his right barely registered before a shadow plowed into him. Will's back crashed into the ground, knocking the air from his lungs. He struggled to catch his breath. Tried to see past the darkness pounding in his eyes. Fought against the weight of a creature he couldn't identify.

Until hands wrapped around his neck.

This was no creature. It was a human. And whoever it was had Will down for the count.

Muscle memory and training rushed through him. Rather than try to dislodge the vise around his neck, Will brought his hands up between his assailant's arms and went for the head. Pressing his palms against the side of his attacker's head, he pressed his thumbs straight into where the eyeballs should be.

An unintelligible growl and a string of muttered curses burnt the air around him. The pressure around his neck eased.

That split second taste of freedom was all he needed. Will gripped his assailant's right arm, then shoved the man's leg back with his elbow, trapping his ankle in his bent knee. Shifting his grip, he grabbed the man's shirt near the shoulder and shoved his right foot against the ground, going into a roll that pitched the man off him.

With a grunt, the attacker rolled away and hopped to his feet, already on the run. The guy was like a ninja— wiry, nimble and fast.

Will scrambled up as well, reaching for his sidearm. He'd take this perp into custody and somehow keep him restrained until backup could get here. He took off in pursuit, but didn't get far before he stumbled to a stop. The guy was outpacing him, and he didn't dare get too far from the plane. This could all be a ruse to lure him away from Jasmine or into a trap. Alone, he couldn't do anything more than let this man get away.

Biting back a frustrated shout, Will ran back to the plane. If nothing else, he could call for backup on the sat phone, although rounding up a helicopter and getting it here at this time of night when no one was injured would likely be a long shot.

In the distance, almost too faint to hear, the sound of an engine roared to life and quickly faded. Likely a four-wheeler.

Either way, the guy was gone.

And all Will had was proof that someone was out to kill him.

SIX

Jasmine sat on the ground near the Twin Otter and let the morning sun warm her in the cool air. On the far side of the plane, Jerry Pace had just opened the engine cover. Although Jasmine had looked over the engine the evening before, she kept her distance now, letting the man work, waiting to see if he confirmed what she'd seen or if he had a good chuckle at her paranoia.

On the far side of the plane, Will stood with Scout at his feet, eyeing his phone. He'd been oddly preoccupied all morning and now he hadn't moved for several minutes, likely reading email or texting with whoever called the shots on his team. The night before, he'd crept into the plane without saying a word to her, retrieved Scout and his backpack, and had never come back. Likely he'd felt safer watching from outside.

Closing her eyes, Jasmine turned her face to the sun, relishing a few moments to herself. The night had been long, especially after his antsy departure, but she'd managed a couple of hours of sleep. It had better be enough to get her through this day and whatever it might have in store. *Lord, let it be smooth air and no more surprises.*

Most of her sleepless night had been spent in deep

conversation with God about Will. The fact that he knew who she really was had flipped her thoughts around and made her feel like she was two different people. The old and the new layered onto each other in ways they hadn't since she'd first entered the program.

The feeling had driven her into some hard-core prayer during the dark night hours. Refuge could be found only in God. And she sure was glad He listened to her.

A shadow darkened the sunlight on her face, and Jasmine eased her eyes open.

"You've got biscuit crumbs on your chin." As he settled to the ground a few feet away from her, Will pointed at her face. "And I've seen ranger students fresh out of the field who ate slower than you just did."

Quirking a smile, Jasmine swiped at her chin, but she didn't have a defense for his comment. She knew she'd put away that ham biscuit quickly, but it was way better than the freeze-dried eggs that were in her emergency stash. "Jerry and his wife cure their own pork. If the man says he's bringing me a biscuit, I eat it quick, before somebody comes tearing out of the wilderness to rip that beauty from my hands." When he had arrived not long after sunrise, in the small Piper Archer he liked to fly, he'd handed her a small cooler of still-warm ham biscuits and a thermos of hot coffee.

Jasmine had wanted to kiss the man on the cheek.

But the older mechanic would never go for that. She settled for a hearty *thank you* while she hugged the cooler to her chest before she let him get to his work. Jerry liked to act gruff, but his concern for her welfare made his tender heart shine bright.

Will cleared his throat and looked toward the low

mountain slope, an odd look on his face, but then he smiled. "I didn't say the food wasn't good. Just that you ate it fast." He took a swig of coffee from one of the metal camping cups Jerry had brought along. "And truth be told, I'd arm wrestle you for the last one if I wasn't such a gentleman. I'm guessing Jerry's wife makes her own biscuits, too?"

"She does. And there's no need to compete. There are still a couple left. Jerry doesn't believe in skimping when it comes to food." Jasmine kept her eyes on the shiny tinfoil of her second biscuit as she unwrapped it. In the morning light, Will's dark hair held auburn highlights that she hadn't noticed before. Something about noticing them made her feel kind of jittery in her stomach. They'd said a lot of things to each other the night before, or at least Will had. Looking at him now—it was like looking at a stranger who she knew too much about.

Or at least looking at someone who ought to be a stranger but *wasn't*. Their long night watching the aurora and talking had shifted the dynamic between them.

Knowing about his mother and his ex-girlfriend made him more real somehow, a man with feelings instead of an authority figure in a blue uniform. He'd endured a lot of pain in his life, and a wounded heart beat beneath the navy coat he wore to ward off the morning's chill.

A heart that needed to heal.

Swallowing hard, Jasmine forcibly tamped down her misfiring emotions. Getting swept up in the fantasy of what it would be like to claim the heart of a man like Will Stryker was just borrowing trouble. She wasn't falling for anybody, not in her situation. From any angle, he represented heartache she definitely didn't need.

She sighed. Part of all this self-awareness meant finding a neutral conversation. "You get all caught up on your emails over there?"

"Emails?" Will unwrapped the biscuit he'd grabbed and looked at her with an arched eyebrow before he nodded. "On my phone just now? That wasn't an email. I was reading the devotion I read every morning. It's the time I set aside for God, and I wasn't going to miss it."

"An appointment with God?"

"Something like that."

Jasmine nodded. She typically did her Bible study first thing in the mornings and spent some time in prayer, but her day was sprinkled with prayer constantly. She assumed Will's was, too.

She'd just taken another bite of biscuit and was savoring the salty ham when Jerry walked over and squatted by her feet. He shoved the toe of her hiking boot with a wrench. "You were right."

Jasmine swallowed quickly, almost choked on a biscuit crumb and had to swig hot coffee before she could answer. With the tears of a burned tongue leaking from the corners of her eyes, she raised an eyebrow. "Right about what?" But even as she said it, she knew.

And she wished she hadn't reached for that second biscuit.

"That fuel line didn't rupture naturally. It's a small cut, not enough to leak out all your fuel at once or burst your line, but enough to drip out what you'd need to make it back home. There's a matching cut in the line on the other engine, too. Both of your tanks are as close to empty as they can get."

Closing her eyes, Jasmine set the biscuit on the ground by her hip. She'd like to rewind thirty seconds, before Jerry had confirmed her worst nightmare.

Beside her, Will moved closer. "Sabotage?" His normally deep voice was gravelly with something Jasmine didn't want to acknowledge. It sounded too much like danger...

And like the end of Jasmine Jefferson.

When she opened her eyes, Jerry was watching her. "You okay?"

"I'm fine." Tossing her biscuit into the cooler, she stood and motioned for the older man to follow her to the plane, away from Will.

He got up and trailed behind them anyway, with Scout close at his heel.

When they reached the plane, she rested a hand on the cold metal next to the open engine. "Why didn't my fuel gauge register the decrease?"

"I don't know." Jerry shoved his cap back and scratched his forehead. His weathered face furrowed into deep rows. "I could tell you maybe it was a bad line with a manufacturing defect and your fuel gauge went on the fritz coincidentally at the same time as your radio, but I don't believe in coincidence. We replaced the fuel line just a couple weeks ago. I'd have noticed a cut, even one that small, and it would have caused a problem before today if I hadn't."

"So the fuel gauge was tampered with as well?" Will looked at the engine as though he understood what he was seeing, but Jasmine guessed he had little idea about the inner workings of a plane engine.

Not that she could do much more than identify the parts herself.

Jerry nodded. "Gas gauges work because there's a float that goes up and down with the gas in the tank. It's hooked to a resistor that sends an electrical impulse from—" He scratched his chin. "Know what? You don't need to know all that. But I'm guessing that when I get this plane back to the hangar, I'm going to find that there's something interesting going on between the resistor and the gauges. Or between the ball and the resistor."

Wrapping her arms around her stomach, Jasmine walked away from the Twin Otter. The plane she'd depended on for two years. She'd flown the others in the small fleet, but this aircraft was the one she loved to pilot the most.

Now it, and maybe someone close to her, had betrayed her.

She drew her lips between her teeth and clamped down. Hard.

Will approached and rested a hand on her back. The move seemed to be instinctual, because his gaze never left Jerry. The lines around his eyes deepened.

Scout moved as well, walking around from Will's left to squeeze between them and lean against Jasmine's leg.

She crouched and petted the collie from his ears down his back, over and over, seeking calm, praying words she couldn't articulate but knew God could understand.

Will stepped closer to Jerry. "Was the plane sabotaged?" He repeated his earlier question, this time with more authority.

"Can't say that for sure. Too many variables." The mechanic took a deep breath and exhaled slowly. "But I can say there's definitely something wrong. And that

if you'd made it over the mountains without a flat place
to land, you two would never have made it back to Fairbanks alive."

Will shifted as much to the right as he could and
kept his mouth shut while Jasmine piloted the smaller
Piper Archer toward Fairbanks. It was early afternoon,
but darkness wouldn't come for a long time. Dinner
wasn't far away, and all he knew was that he wanted
a huge cheeseburger and some distance from Jasmine
Jefferson.

Earlier, while Jerry had stayed behind to repair the
Twin Otter the best he could in the bush, Jasmine and
Will had taken off in his tiny plane. They'd made a short
hop to the small village of Winchinechen to drop off a
load of cargo that Jerry had brought with him. Bringing cargo along with him minimized the number of
flights into the bush. They'd returned to follow Jerry
back to Fairbanks, and he now flew ahead of them in
the Twin Otter.

This plane was smaller than the other plane, but the
noise level was low enough that they could talk without the radios. That was the good thing, although he
certainly wasn't about to tell her he'd been attacked the
night before. He needed to huddle with his team about
that. And soon.

The bad thing was, no matter what Will had done
all day, his elbow and his shoulder had collided with
Jasmine's. Normally, he'd let such incidental contact
slide, but today...

Today it made him feel things. Each time they
touched, his heart reminded him of how he'd opened
up to her the night before. How sky and land and dis-

tance had combined to coax him into pouring out things he'd never really talked about to another human being.

He'd been puzzling how that had happened since the plane bounced along the ground and lifted into the air earlier this morning, and he still couldn't decide if that was a good thing or a bad thing. All he knew for sure was that it was uncomfortable.

And it wasn't where his focus should be. At some point yesterday, either before she left Fairbanks or at one of her stops, someone had sabotaged Jasmine's plane and hunted them down on the frontier. Was she the target?

Or was *he*?

Jasmine was clearly thinking as well, because she'd been equally quiet.

The day had been interminably long and now, with only about twenty minutes before they reached Fairbanks, Will wasn't sure if he could handle the silence any longer. "What's on your mind?"

Jasmine looked at him, but sunglasses hid her eyes. She had the earpiece of her headset closest to him behind her ear so she could hear both him and the radio. With a sigh, she checked the radio's settings then lifted the mic from her mouth. "Everything is on my mind. But none of it is what you think it is."

Everything. Those two syllables encompassed a lot. But if none of it was what he was thinking, then it couldn't be the false tip or the sabotage. "It's been a pretty interesting couple of days."

She nodded once and drew her lower lip between her teeth.

Something was clearly bugging her, and it was a lot

more than she was willing to admit. "So what are you biting your lip to keep from saying?"

This time, she smiled and graced him with a short chuckle. "Well, this morning I was quiet because I was focused on the plane. I haven't flown anything except the Twin Otter in a while. Had to get my small plane brain into place."

"And now?"

"Look, Will." She made a quick sweep of the gauges. "Nobody knows me. Literally *nobody*. When it comes to my family, I might as well be dead, because I can never contact them again. Everyone else knows this manufactured person who doesn't exist outside of files the government invented. Do you have any idea what that feels like?"

"No." It had been one thing for him to move from Minnesota to Alaska, where everyone was a stranger. But at least he'd been able to come as himself.

"It's like being a walking, talking, breathing character out of a novel. I'm an invention. A fabricated creation. It's surreal, because I'm still me with my thoughts and my memories, but that person doesn't exist in the real world. I have to be careful about what I say. It's like my past isn't real. There are mornings when I wake up and literally don't know who I am. It really messes with my head."

Will opened his mouth to try to fix it, but then he stopped. He couldn't begin to relate to what Jasmine was going through.

She sighed and tipped her head toward the ceiling. "I've said way too much to you, more than I should have and more than is safe. It's so bizarre that, right now, you feel like my only friend."

As Scout pressed his head into Will's palm, loving the ear scratch, Will felt his breath grow easier. Sometimes his partner was as much a therapy dog as he was a sniffer. "When you face death together and then get forced to spend the night in the wilderness, it can start you talking."

"I guess." There was a tone in her voice that sounded a little bit like hurt.

Will could slap himself in the forehead. She'd been talking about friendship and he'd made it sound like circumstance. She'd laid her heart bare in this cockpit, and he'd managed to deflect her emotion straight into the empty sky.

The same emotion he was feeling. Because the conversation they'd shared and the things he'd felt while talking to her meant way more than he'd ever imagined. He was drawn to her personality and her bravery and her candidness. And while he wasn't sure what would happen between them once the plane landed in Fairbanks, he knew he couldn't just walk away and leave her behind. Already, it would be like detaching his arm.

This was definitely weird.

He wanted her to know this was more to him, but there was no way to say it without sounding like an awkward cable TV movie. He scratched Scout under the chin. "So, your past? What's your family like?"

"Mom's an investment banker. Dad's a teacher. My brother is a ranger." She sniffed, and her grip tightened on the yoke. "I guess all of that's still true. I don't even dare do an internet search to see what they're up to, though the marshals would tell me if anything major happened."

If only he could show her photos on social media or

have Eli do a search to check on them. That was impossible, though. Any sort of digging could lead someone straight to her.

Still, he wished he could do something for the woman who'd forgiven him for assuming she was a criminal and who'd listened to his sad story.

A story that had marked him for years. Had colored every decision he'd made. Had kept him from trusting anyone with the truth.

Until now.

Will straightened in the seat so suddenly that Scout tensed beneath his fingers.

Trust. At some point, he'd stopped suspecting Jasmine was a criminal. Instead, he'd trusted her with the true story of his life. Without hesitation. Without fear of rejection or judgment. Without considering that there might be consequences.

He *trusted* Jasmine Jefferson.

The realization tilted his world as surely as if she had banked the plane into a hard right.

"What's wrong?" She leaned forward slightly in the small space. "There are airsick bags in the door pocket."

Their close proximity meant she'd felt his realization as surely as if he'd reached for her hand. He breathed in and out twice, righting himself. Better to let her think the issue was physical and not emotional. "I'm fine. Just felt a little bit of instability." Yeah, that was the perfect explanation. "So, what does the rest of your day look like?"

"It's technically my day off. I don't fly again for a couple of days." She banked the plane at the outskirts of Fairbanks. The airfield was probably only five or so minutes away. "You're welcome to ride along again when I go up since we really didn't find anything on this outing."

He *needed* to go with her for the investigation. But more than that, he *wanted* to go with her for the company. As she'd expressed earlier, she knew him. It seemed impossible, but she did. "I'll have a talk with my team, but since this investigation is my primary focus at the moment, I'll probably take you up on the offer." He also needed to determine how much protection she might need after being seen with him.

"Sounds like a plan." Jasmine pulled the headset fully onto both ears and tuned the radio. She identified her aircraft as a Piper, rattled off some numbers, then conducted a brief discussion about winds and approach.

Almost before Will was ready, she'd settled the plane gently to the ground and coasted to a stop by a grounds crewman who guided her to a stop outside the hangar. She removed her headset and ran her fingers through the ends of her hair. "Thank you for flying with Kesuk Aviation, Trooper." The words held slight humor, and her grin was the most relaxed he'd seen.

"I'll definitely fly with you again. And I'll leave a five-star review online."

Jasmine wrinkled her nose, then motioned for him to open the door, which was on his side of the plane.

As he shoved the door open, a gunshot echoed across the airfield and a bullet cracked into the windshield.

SEVEN

Jasmine shrieked and froze, gaze fixed on the webbed windshield that had nearly shattered at the impact. Her breath caught in her chest. Everything stopped moving and her ears roared.

"Jasmine!" The fierce growl in Will's voice shook her from her fog. He reached across the narrow plane and pulled her as low as he could in the small space as the sound of another shot ricocheted off metal.

Her head crashed into his chest, and something stung at her hairline. Had she been shot?

The weight of Will's arm lay heavy across her shoulders, and her body screamed at the unnatural position as they attempted to stay below the windows. "What just happened? Is someone shooting at us?"

As if to answer her question, another shot echoed across the airfield, but there was no answering strike to the plane.

Hand on his pistol at his hip, Will shifted as though he was trying to shield her from the threat outside. "Looks like. You're not hurt, are you?"

From where he was secured behind Will's seat, Scout yapped once, the bark shrill in the enclosed space.

Pulling in a shallow breath, Jasmine tried to make herself as small as possible in the cramped space so that Will could have cover as well. "I think I'm okay." The answer was relative. While she was still breathing, the pain in her temple screamed she'd been hit by something. Her emotions and fears had definitely taken a direct hit. She was shaking and sweat trickled down her temple, probably mixed with blood.

From outside, shouts passed between buildings on the airfield, but none drew closer to the plane. Likely, everyone had taken cover.

"We're going to be fine." Will's words were low, meant to soothe.

They didn't. How were they going to be fine? Someone out there, hidden where she couldn't see them, had aimed at her and fired. This was a repeat of her past, the very thing she'd come to Alaska to avoid.

Jasmine huddled deeper into the seat, but there was nowhere to move. The interior of the plane was too warm. Will's arm across her shoulders and back was too heavy. She couldn't breathe. Her temple pounded.

Her very worst nightmare had burst from her brain into the daylight. How often had she awoken at night in a cold sweat from visions of hidden assailants dragging her into the darkness?

She fought to control her breathing. It felt as if everything inside of her wanted to burst through her skin and run. She had to—

Will rested his chin on the top of her head. "It's okay. I'm here. Scout's here. I promise we're going to get out of this. The guy hasn't fired in a couple of minutes and, if he's smart, he's already gone."

There was no way he could possibly know that everything was going to be fine or if the shooter was still out there, but something about the tone of his words and the warmth of his touch seeped into her screaming mind. Even though it seemed impossible, she believed him.

"Trust me?" He whispered the words against her hair.

Pursing her lips, Jasmine exhaled slowly and nodded.

"Okay." He pulled away and eased up to look out the spiderwebbed front window.

It took everything Jasmine had inside of her not to jerk him back down again. If someone had a rifle and a scope out there Will was making himself an easy target.

But as quickly as he lifted his head, he leaned over her again. "It sounded like the shot came from the front, possibly from the tree line at the far end of the runway. I'd think anyone willing to shoot at us would be smart enough to get away from the scene before law enforcement can get here. Someone's bound to have called the—"

Shouts from outside cut him off. Resting his hand on Jasmine's head again to remind her to stay down, he rose up slightly and peered out the window.

The voices grew louder, calling her name.

Recognizable voices. "That's Keith and Darrin. My bosses." Jasmine moved to sit up, but Will stopped her.

"I'm not saying we're in the clear. Whoever was taking potshots wanted me or you. Just because he's not firing at anyone right now, that doesn't mean for certain he's gone. We need a plan." He muttered something under his breath, then leaned across Jasmine toward the side window. "State trooper! Get back inside! Now! And stay there!"

The voices outside stopped, then feet thudded away from the plane.

At least they'd obeyed and were out of harm's way.

"Okay, I've changed my mind. We're not waiting it out in here. There's not enough room to stay low." Will pulled away and glanced out the side window. "We're not that far from the hangar, and I don't see another plane inside. Can you restart the aircraft and get us inside?"

"Maybe. But no plane likes to be restarted right after shutdown." She could flood the engine and leave them in even worse shape.

The silence outside was terrifying, worse than a volley of gunshots could ever be. Had the man left? Was he moving into a better position? Were there crosshairs trained on her right now?

Or were they trained on Will?

With her mind focused on desperate prayers for the plane to start and for safety, Jasmine twisted in the seat and tried to keep herself as small as possible in the cramped space. With a flick of switches and a check of gauges, she held her breath.

The engine fired.

Though her muscles threatened to turn her into a puddle on the floor, she released the brake and eased the plane slowly into a turn, rolling toward the hangar as fast as she dared.

Three more shots. Three more *thwacks* into the plane.

Jasmine gasped and her joints locked. The skin of the plane wasn't that thick. A bullet could pierce it and hit one of them at any second. She couldn't do this. She couldn't get them out of this.

It all ended right here.

Will's hand rested on her wrist, behind where her frozen fingers gripped the yoke. "Jas, you can do this." His voice was low and calm, his hand warm on her skin. "I know you can do this. It's just a few more feet."

This man didn't have to be here. He didn't have to lay his life on the line for her. Will could have ditched her yesterday, could have called in a chopper and left her stranded in the wilderness alone the night before.

But he'd stuck by her. And now, for the second time in two days, she held his life in her hands.

This wasn't all about her. Other lives were at stake. She'd get the plane into the hangar. She'd get both Will and Scout to safety.

Or she'd die trying.

Will didn't breathe again until the shadow of the hangar's interior darkened the sunlight in the cockpit. Jasmine had done it. Despite her terror, she had guided them to safety.

Again.

The same man who'd guided them to a stop earlier ducked out from behind the shelter of the hangar wall and slid the door closed behind them.

Will slumped in his seat. For now, they were safe. But there was no telling how long that would last. He straightened and tried to scan the dimly lit hangar.

Beside him, Jasmine leaned forward and rested her head on the yoke. For a moment, she was so still that Will thought she'd lost consciousness, but then her hair trembled where it covered her face. Her shoulders followed, and the shaking grew exponentially worse than it had been earlier.

Adrenaline crash. Will rested a hand on her back, wishing there was a way to pull her closer in the tiny cockpit, but the danger wasn't over.

"You guys okay?" a voice called out and the door next to Will popped open. When he turned, the man from the grounds crew stood in the open doorway peering in.

"We're good. You?" Will kept one hand protectively on Jasmine's back and one wrapped tight around the grip of the holstered Sig. The man had guided them to a stop and secured the building behind them, but that didn't mean he was one of the good guys. Right now, anyone who came within a mile of Jasmine was his number one suspect.

"I may need a heart checkup after this, but I'm good." The crewman noticed Jasmine, and his face crumpled. "Jas get hit?"

"No. Just recovering."

Her back tensed beneath his fingers as she pulled in a deep breath, then she sat up and leaned across Will. She laid a hand on the older man's arm. "I'm fine, Brandt. Something grazed my forehead, that's all. Just shook up."

"You're bleeding." Brandt looked around as if he could conjure up an ambulance and EMTs.

Will whipped his head to look at Jasmine, nearly crashing into her forehead as she sat back in her seat. A tiny rivulet of blood ran from her hairline.

Her hand went to her temple. "Something hit me but… I wasn't shot, was I?" Her eyes met Will's and narrowed in confusion and fear.

His mind raced through the moments of the attack and after, and his hand went to the badge on his chest. "My badge. You hit it on the way down."

Her lips parted slightly in understanding, and she looked at Brandt. Slowly, a calm seemed to overtake her, almost as though she was more concerned with the other man's emotions than with her physical well-being. She offered him a slight smile. "I'm fine."

She wasn't fine because of anything Will had done. After the suspected sabotage of the plane and the subsequent attempt on his life, he should have been more vigilant, should have had his eyes open. He definitely shouldn't have been distracted by Jasmine's talk of friendship and healing and all of those other things he hadn't realized he craved until she came into his life.

And there he went again, missing the point. "Jasmine, how well do you know Brandt?"

For a split second, the crewman looked insulted, but then his expression softened. He remained silent, waiting for Jasmine to speak.

"He's been here longer than I have. He's safe." Paling, she turned toward Brandt. "Where's Jerry?"

The mechanic had landed just a few minutes ahead of them. Had he been targeted as well?

"He was in the other hangar when the shooting started. They locked themselves in there. He's fine." Brandt pulled away slightly to look at Will. "I called 911 and locked up this place tight, too. Nobody's getting in. You should be safe now."

Will eyed Brandt. If the man had plans to kill Jasmine, he'd have done it by now. He had no choice but to trust her opinion of the man and to trust the man himself. Will slowly secured his pistol. With a soft command, he reached back and patted Scout on the head, giving the dog permission to stand down.

Brandt watched with interest.

When Scout relaxed, Will pulled his hand back and focused on the crewman. He had to get out of this plane so he could survey the hanger and have more space to get a good look at Jasmine's injury. "You're on a ladder?"

"Yep."

"Okay, I'm going to step out and help get Jasmine out of here. Do you have a first-aid kit?"

Brandt jerked a thumb over his shoulder. "In the locker over there. I'll go get it."

Will nodded his assent, then focused on Jasmine. "Are you ready to get out of here?"

She nodded with a loud exhale, then dropped her head back against the seat and stared at the ceiling. It was obvious that the adrenaline ebb and emotional crash were slamming her hard.

At least he hoped that was all that was wrong.

Will climbed out of the plane. Two bullet holes marred the metal below his window. So close. *Too close*. The one that had nearly shattered the window had likely come within inches of ending one of their lives.

No time to think of that at the moment. His first order of business was to make sure she was safe.

He reached across the seats and helped Jasmine from the plane and to the ground. He accepted the first-aid kit from Brandt and then assisted her into a chair that the older man had wheeled over.

"Can you find us a bottle of water or something?" The last thing Will needed was the man breathing down his neck or having to worry that maybe he wasn't so trustworthy after all.

With a nod, Brandt jogged over to a small cabinet on the other side of the hangar.

In the distance, sirens wailed, growing closer by the second.

Good. Backup was on the way.

Will cracked open the case and rested it in Jasmine's lap.

For the first time, she met his eye. "You bring too much adventure into my life, Trooper."

Relief almost made him drop the antiseptic wipe he'd pulled from the kit. If she could crack a joke, she was going to be okay. "Yeah?" He drew on a glove, ripped open the antiseptic and gently tipped her chin so he could get a good look at her temple. "I could say the same about you. I may have been shot at before, but I've never narrowly avoided a plane crash in the bush."

She smiled, then winced as he dabbed at the wound.

"Sorry." The cut was small, but it had to sting. "It's not bad. It's already pretty much stopped bleeding." He grabbed gauze and wiped the blood from her cheek. "Looks like I'm a bigger danger than the shooter was. Sorry."

His fingers still rested on her chin, and they moved when she shook her head. "Danger?" Her eyes caught his, a haunted look darkening her expression. "What if I've been found? What if I have to start over again?"

The fear in her eyes was too much for him. In that instant, Jasmine became his to protect. He had brought this violence into her life, and he would watch over her until the threat was gone.

"That would be too coincidental." He slid his hand to the back of her neck and pulled her head to his chest. "I'm going to make sure you're safe."

As the sirens echoed off the buildings, Will hoped that was a promise he could keep.

EIGHT

Jasmine sat in Keith's office with her elbows on her knees and her head buried in her hands. She stared at the tile beneath her feet. The dingy gray seemed to pulse with the beat of her pounding heart.

Wouldn't it be ironic if she dropped dead from the stress and saved whoever had attacked them the trouble?

Not quite two feet away, Scout sat with his back to her and his eyes on the door while Will stood in the hallway, talking in low tones with another trooper who'd arrived with another K-9.

She'd always wanted a dog, but having one by her side who was ordered to guard her wasn't exactly the way she'd imagined. In her daydreams, there had been more camping and stick throwing and less gunfire and drug smuggling.

Lord, what have I gotten myself into? Jasmine's eyes slipped shut.

All she'd done for the past hour was pray while it seemed every one of Alaska's finest patrolled the area around the airport.

Because of her.

Please don't let this be about my testimony. I don't

want to leave. She couldn't bear to walk away from flying or from the people she was privileged to serve. There was no doubt in her mind what she was called to do with her new life, and turning her back on it felt wrong.

A lump rose to her throat. She didn't have it in her to once again become another person when she'd only just begun to feel comfortable as this one.

"I brought your backpack in." Twin thuds hit the floor, then the couch beside her sank and a hand rested gently on her back. "You doing okay?" Will's low voice was as warm as his touch. Both brought a measure of peace that they really shouldn't.

"Somebody shot at me." The bitterness in her voice wasn't intentional. It was simply there, welling up from deep in her gut.

"Yeah, that was probably not the smartest question to ask." He moved his hand slightly from side to side. "It's not the best day of your life when that happens."

"Nope."

"Well, the good news is that the shooter isn't out there. We found where he drove up. Looks like he fired from the window of a car, because we have tire tracks and shell casings but no footprints."

Jasmine sighed. "The bad news is he got away." Which meant he was still out there, ready to try to strike again.

"Our crime scene techs are measuring tire tracks. They'll look for prints on the shell casings. It's only a matter of time before he's in custody and we know exactly what's going on." His hand paused its soft motion on her back. "I talked to Deputy Marshal Maldonado."

Jasmine's heart lurched. This was it. The moment

when her life shredded once again. She couldn't even make her throat push forth the words to ask what he'd said.

It almost seemed as though Will understood. He slipped his hand to her opposite shoulder and drew her close, his voice so low she could barely hear it. "He's put his entire team to work on your case. So far, there's no indication that you're being targeted or that your identity has been compromised."

Goose bumps raised on her arms. Her heart tugged toward him. He was close. Really close.

Of course, he was also saying exactly what she wanted to hear, so the softness in her emotions probably had more to do with relief than with the man bringing the news.

Will's chin moved against the top of her head. "That shot came so quickly, it's doubtful the shooter even had time to determine who he was aiming at. He went for the first movement he saw. My team and I are still operating on the theory that this is about me being on the plane with you. That I'm the target." He gave her shoulder a quick squeeze then pulled away. "You don't have to do this. I can fly with anyone. We have our own planes. It doesn't have to be—"

"I want to do this." Jasmine shoved to her feet and walked over to Keith's desk, staring down at his papers without actually seeing them. "You can fly out there all you want with your pilots, but when you get into some of the remote villages, they aren't going to talk to you." She faced Will, who was looking up at her, his face etched with deep lines of concern. "You should consider going in civilian clothes. Might make it easier on you."

His jaw tightened, and he studied something over her head. "I don't—"

A door slammed.

Jasmine jumped, her knees nearly betraying her.

"What about my plane?" Down the hall, Keith's shout punctuated the crash from the door. "I have a Piper Archer sitting in my hangar with a cracked windscreen and looking like Swiss cheese. I can't get it off the ground and use it for deliveries until it's been declared airworthy again. Who's going to pay for that?"

Will was on his feet, and so was Scout. Both faced the door.

A lower voice drifted behind Keith's bluster. "We can sit down and talk about that later. We'll make sure you have an official report that you can use to contact your insurance company, and—"

"That's not helping me today is it? The fool shot up my plane." Keith stormed into the small office. "I want it fixed." He stopped short when he saw Jasmine, his eyes wide. His mouth opened slightly, and he glanced from her to Will, then back over his shoulder to the trooper behind him, the one Will had been speaking to earlier. "Jasmine." Keith's shoulders slumped and he stared at the ceiling, regret edging his expression. His voice dropped. "Were you hurt?"

Had it really taken him having to face her to ask that question? Two years of working for him and his plane came first? Glancing at Will, who was watching Keith, she swallowed the words she wanted to say. "Just a scratch on my forehead." From Will's badge, not from the shooter.

"I'm sorry about the rant." Her boss pulled her into a brotherly hug and let go quickly. "It's easier to worry about the plane than what might have happened if that guy had better aim."

Jasmine's knees still wobbled. She planted her hand on the desk by the printed flight schedule. Keith had always been more business minded and less emotional, so it made sense he'd run from anything that scared him. She forgave his *plane first* attitude.

If only the plane was all *she* had to worry about.

"I wish I knew what was going on." Keith looked at each of them in turn. "Our safety record at Kesuk Aviation is impeccable. Now I have a shooting on my airfield and, according to Jerry, a plane that's been tampered with. Nothing like this ever happened before you came on the scene, Troopers." Picking up a pen, he tapped it on the desk, eyeing Will. "You won't be flying with Jasmine again."

Before Will could speak, she squared her shoulders. "No." Her boss could think whatever he wanted. It was his business to run after all. But she wasn't ready to cut ties with Will or his investigation. If she was going down, she was going down fighting for the people she cared about.

Five pairs of eyes swung toward her—three male and one canine.

Keith was the first to speak. "*No*, what?"

Will's arched eyebrow echoed Keith's question.

"I want Trooper Stryker to fly with me." She needed to go with him and, after the chaos of the past twenty-four hours, she needed him to be with her.

The pen's tapping ceased. Keith's lips tightened, and he seemed to try to read her mind.

Jasmine met his gaze and held it, refusing to back down. While she was well-known for being one of the friendliest pilots around, she was also well-known for being one of the most stubborn.

"You were shot at because of him." He shook his head and dropped the pen to the desk with a clatter. "I'm not going to have you flying into danger. And, not that this is as important as you, but Darrin and I can't afford to have any more planes damaged."

"You can't prove this is about the trooper." She bit her lip. She'd almost said too much. Her mind scrambled to backtrack.

"Jasmine's already been seen with me." Will stepped to her side, his shoulder brushing hers in a subtle show of support. He had her back. Despite the fact that he'd tried to back out of flying with her, he was going to honor her wishes. "Anyone who wants to come at us is going to come at her, assuming she's acting as my eyes, even if I'm not with her."

"And they'd be right." Jasmine crossed her arms over her chest.

"She's safer if I'm with her. At least she'll have someone watching her back." Will tilted his head, aiming his chin at Scout, who rested at his heel. "Make that two someones."

Keith picked up the pen and started tapping again.

"You're already short a pilot because of Manny's surgery." Jasmine stepped closer to the desk. "You don't want me to step away because I feel unsafe without Trooper Stryker at my side, do you?"

For the briefest second, Keith's expression hardened, but then he tossed the pen across the desk and crossed his arms, mimicking Jasmine's posture. "Darrin and I will discuss it."

"He's flying with me, Keith." Jasmine brushed past

Will, headed for the door. "And I'm going home." The exhaustion dumped on her like the sudden squall had the day before. In the time it took her to reach the door and step past the other trooper, her entire body felt like it doubled in weight. She craved her bed and the hours of sleep she'd been robbed of the night before.

She was at the door to the enclosed entryway before Will and the other trooper caught up. He reached around her and grabbed the handle before she could walk out. "Wait."

Waiting was the last thing she wanted to do. "Will, I want to go home. Please. You can meet me back here the next time I fly. I'll text you the flight details."

"You can't just go charging out into the world. Someone shot at you—at *us*—today." Will eased between Jasmine and the door. "Let Sean and me check your vehicle and ours, then we'll walk out with you. We'll follow you home and make sure everything there is secure, okay?" He slipped her backpack from his shoulder and held it out to her, his expression commanding, but with a slight plea.

She jerked the bag from his hand. "Really?" She didn't need a babysitter or a bodyguard.

Or maybe she did. It was nice to be all tough-girl bravado like she was some action movie hero, but the truth was she was simply a regular woman who barely knew who she was. While she'd like to think she could take down an assailant with her bare hands, past history already said she could not.

"Fine. You can escort me, but once you know my house is safe, we're done for the day."

With a lingering look, Will walked into the enclosed entry, his head swiveling from side to side.

Scout took up his place beside her as though he knew exactly what was going on, and Sean and his K-9 fell in behind them.

Their presence ought to make her feel comforted and safe.

But the fact remained that someone had sabotaged her plane and had opened fire at her.

She'd never felt more trapped.

"We're checking her car and following her back to her home?" Trooper Sean West cast a quick look to where Jasmine waited inside the enclosed entry to the building, then bent down to look under her car.

Will gently opened the driver's-side door and scanned the interior. Nothing looked out of place. He'd refused to let Jasmine get into her car until he and Sean checked it out to make sure no one had tampered with it. Whoever had taken those shots wasn't playing.

Neither was he.

Right about now, he wished he had Trooper Maya Rodriguez and her explosive-sniffing partner Sarge by his side. Sure, he and Sean were good friends. His Japanese Akita Inu partner, Grace, was an amazing K-9, but she was a cadaver dog who was frequently called on in avalanches. Her nose was awesome, but it wasn't trained for explosives.

Same with Scout. It was too bad drugs were no longer his primary concern.

"You ignoring me or are you totally absorbed in your work?" Sean's voice was laced with sarcasm, belying his amusement.

The situation wasn't amusing. "Let's just say I'm not a fan of her being unprotected after everything that happened the past two days. Let's also say there's more going on than you realize." Will didn't want to divulge any more of Jasmine's secret than he had to. At the moment, his teammate didn't need to know. "I'm leaning heavily toward Jasmine being shot at because of my presence, but there could be some underlying factors."

"Care to share?" Crossing his arms, Sean leaned them on the top of Jasmine's Subaru as Will straightened.

"If it becomes need to know, then yes." When the other man's eyebrow arched, Will exhaled roughly. He owed his friend more, but there wasn't a lot he could offer. "Look, I'm not trying to be vague. It's not my story to tell. Just trust me on this one."

"No problem." Sean pushed away from the car. "You want backup from me?"

Will tapped the top of the vehicle and tightened his lips. It certainly wouldn't hurt. "You're not on an assignment?"

"Not at the moment. The Missing Bride case is still ongoing, but until we get a new tip, we're busy digging into what we already have."

While their specialized team had assignments all over the state, Violet James's was never far from their minds. With little new evidence, the case was in danger of growing cold, and Violet was in danger of being lost forever.

No one in their unit wanted to see that happen.

"What about Katie's family and the reindeer ranch?" Their colonel's assistant, Katie Kapowski, had presented them with another mystery, one they were working in their rare spare time. Her aunt's reindeer sanctuary had been the victim of several attacks. A DNA match to evidence found at the scene suggested someone in the family, although Katie insisted her only living relative was her aunt.

Sean tapped his fist against his thigh. "There's new intel there. Brayden Ford had a talk with Katie's aunt Addie. Turns out, she has a brother named Terence that Katie never knew about. He took off years ago. Eli's trying to get a location on him now."

Eli was a busy man. "Why would Addie lie about having a brother?"

Sean shrugged. "Who knows? We all know that family can be weird. Brayden's still working that angle, so he should have some answers soon. It's kind of thrown Katie for a loop. Here she's thought all this time it was only her and Addie, and all the while, there's been an uncle." Scratching his chin, he tipped his head toward Scout. "In more pressing issues, are you paying attention to your partner?"

Had something happened to Scout? Will jerked his head down and found his partner sitting at his heel, waiting patiently while the men talked. "He's fine."

"He's also not alerting."

Sean was right. According to Scout's super sniffer, there had never been drugs in or around Jasmine's car. If there had been, he'd either be pawing at the spot where they were hidden or he'd be sitting differently, in a passive alert. As it was, his partner was completely unconcerned. If there had been any reason to doubt Jasmine's innocence, the complete absence of drugs or their residue in her vehicle was a mark in her favor.

It was also a reminder they had to get her safely home. They could talk more about their cases later. "Jasmine gave me her address. I'll put it in the GPS and take the lead. She'll be behind me, and you can follow. I'm fairly certain I'm the target, but I meant what I said in the office. Now that she's working with us, she's as vulnerable as we are." He prayed what he was saying was true. If he'd done something to jeopardize her identity, he'd never be able to forgive himself.

After another quick survey of the area, he escorted Jasmine from the building to her car. As she dropped her bag in the passenger seat and buckled in, he rested one hand on the door and the other on the roof, leaning in to talk to her. He filled her in on the plan for the drive. "When we get there, I want to go in first, just to be safe."

She looked around Will to where Sean had secured Grace in his SUV and now sat in the driver's seat, waiting for them to roll out. She lowered her voice. "I came to Alaska to avoid situations like this."

"I know. It's fine with me if you pretend we're just doing this for my peace of mind more than for your well-being." He flashed her a smile that she echoed, if only for a second.

For the briefest moment, he wondered what it would be like to stand at her door like this and carry on a normal conversation, one that didn't involve drugs and shooters and law enforcement. One that was about dinner or movies or—

Nope. He reset his thinking and pulled away from the door. There was no sense in wondering what it would be like to date her or even to be real friends with her. Their interaction was going to be brief and would end soon. He'd move on to other things, and she'd continue her flights into the bush, helping people survive.

Tapping the top of the car twice, he shut the door

then walked over to his SUV. The Alaska State Troopers logo clearly identified who he was, while Alaska K-9 Unit in blue lettering to the left of the rear windows and on the back let the world know Scout was on board. He opened the back, gestured for Scout to jump into his climate-controlled kennel, then secured the vehicle.

The drive to Jasmine's was short, only about ten minutes, but it was one of the tensest Will had ever driven. He'd protected witnesses before and had once even been on an escort detail for a visiting vice president, but this? *This* felt like a personal investment. As though Jasmine's life was squarely in his hands. And while losing anyone on his watch was unthinkable, he somehow had the feeling that losing Jasmine would be devastating.

Will scrubbed his hand down his face. The attack last night had rattled him more than he wanted to admit. Operating on pretty much no sleep coupled with the tension of the last twenty-four hours was making him loopy. Once he'd rested and grabbed a shower and had a decent meal, his emotions would fall back into line and he'd remember the truth… That Jasmine Jefferson was another person he'd encountered on the job. Nothing more.

Forcing himself to focus on the task at hand, he kept his eyes moving as he scanned the road in front of him and the side streets that fed into the main road. The last thing he needed was someone roaring out to clip Jasmine from between his vehicle and Sean's.

He exhaled slowly as he turned into the parking lot of her condo. The long, low structure was older, but it had been updated with modern stone accents and well-tended landscaping.

Pulling into a parking space, he motioned for Jasmine to wait when she stopped beside him.

Sean parked on her side.

Will caught Sean's eye above her car and, in silent agreement, they both slowly exited their vehicles and made a quick survey of the area. Nothing seemed to be out of place, but the sooner he had her inside and safely behind the locked door of her condo, the calmer he'd feel.

He leashed Scout and let his partner out of his kennel, then walked to Jasmine's car. "Ready?"

"I feel like the president with a Secret Service detail." She shouldered her bag, slipped out of the car and shut the door. "Like before I testified." Her expression was taut.

This must be resurrecting terrible memories of why she'd run. Will had seen people die, and those horrid images still woke him up at night. It had to be even more traumatic for a civilian.

Instead of hugging her, he rested a hand on her back and ushered her forward. "Let me have your key. I'll unlock the door."

She passed him a ring. "The big one opens the outside door. The second opens my condo on the second floor, at the opposite end of the hall from the elevator."

"We'll take the elevator then." Too much could go wrong in a stairwell. He stepped around her and headed for the building.

Sean met them at the sidewalk. He and Grace tucked in behind.

No one was in the small entry, and the elevator ride was silent.

On the second floor, Will walked out first. He scanned

the hallway, a straight line to a large window at the end, next to Jasmine's condo. The walls were off-white and the floor was carpeted in blue-gray. At regular intervals, blue doors stood closed.

Seeing no threat and nowhere for anyone to hide, he motioned his tiny crew out of the elevator. They walked to the end of the hall in an awkward line, like kindergarteners on the first day of school.

As they neared Jasmine's door, Will halted. Resting his right hand on his pistol grip, he held his left behind him to stop Jasmine and Sean from proceeding.

"What's wrong?" Her whisper was loud in the silence, but then she gasped.

Ten feet away, the door to her condo stood partially opened.

NINE

"Secure Jasmine." Will drew his pistol and barked the order to Sean.

Jasmine reached out to wrap her fingers into the back of Will's shirt, but Sean grabbed her arm and pulled her into the corner.

Will and Scout disappeared into her condo.

Please, God... There was nothing more. Just the frantic prayer that no one was inside to hurt them.

Sean stood in front of her, weapon drawn, his K-9 at attention by his side. They watched the hallway toward the elevator, then he tilted his head toward a door to their left. "Stairwell?"

"Yes."

"Not quite ready to risk getting trapped in there... or with leaving Will without backup."

Will. He'd gone into her condo alone.

Maybe she'd simply forgotten to shut the door yesterday. Even though she always locked the deadbolt and checked twice.

This couldn't be happening. This had to be a nightmare. There was no way her fuel line had been cut and her plane riddled with bullet holes *and* her condo broken into. Coincidence was out the window.

So was the idea that any of this was about Will's investigation. She was clearly the target.

An eternity passed in crawling seconds before Will's voice rang out. "Clear!" It was only a moment later when he appeared in her doorway, holstering his pistol. "No one is here." He addressed Sean, but faced Jasmine. "There was someone inside before we arrived." Will stepped away from the door and held out a hand for her to enter.

Sean and Grace followed.

She steeled herself as she brushed past Will, but no amount of preparation could ready her for the sight. Her backpack slipped from her fingers and crunched her toe.

She winced, the physical pain jerking her into the truth that this was no nightmare. This was an awful, shattered reality.

Nothing was in its place. Couch cushions, furniture, photos… Everything had been pulled from walls and cabinets and thrown to the floor. "Why?" Her hands shook. She wrapped them around her stomach and tried to hold herself together. "Who hates me this much?" Besides the obvious.

But something didn't fit. If it was about the case that had landed her in WITSEC, surely whoever had broken in would have waited to kill her. Trashing her apartment was a pointless exercise for a hired killer who would want to leave as little evidence behind as possible.

Not that it mattered. Someone had destroyed her safe space. The one place she felt secure outside of an airplane. Within these walls, she'd had the freedom to be her real, authentic self. The outside world knew Jasmine Jefferson. But in here, Yasmine Carlisle still lived.

Until now.

Her entire body and mind went numb. No thoughts, no emotions, no feeling. Nothing. Just empty deadness from the outside in.

Something brushed her leg, pulling her out of her stupor, and Scout slipped past her. He sniffed the edges of the room, then roamed the floor with his nose down before he dropped into the exact middle of her living room, next to the overturned coffee table, and sat perfectly still with his nose in the air.

"What's wrong?" Jasmine took a step back and collided with Will's chest. Had Scout scented something? Was someone still in the apartment?

With a heavy sigh, Will laid a hand on her back for a brief second, then edged around her to Scout. He gave a command Jasmine couldn't hear, and Scout dutifully trotted into her open kitchen, where he repeated the same actions and ended up sitting in the middle of the floor among her scattered utensils.

"Will?"

He eyed Scout before he turned to Jasmine. Hesitating, he glanced over her head at Sean, who had come inside and closed the door. "He's alerting. There aren't drugs present at the moment, but whoever was in here and wrecked the place either had them on him or had interacted with them recently." The way he studied her was odd, but then he pulled in a deep breath and looked away.

Jasmine tilted her head toward the ceiling, relief and fear warring inside her. If this was about drugs, then this was about Will's case, not about her identity.

But that didn't let her off the hook. Someone was still targeting her, likely because she was working with Will. She tipped her chin toward Scout. "How does he do that?"

"Super sniffer." Will flashed a grim smile. "And a lot of training." He pulled a chew toy out of his backpack and carried it over to the border collie, whose tail thumped wildly on the floor. After a brief tug of war, Scout curled up to chew on what was clearly his favorite treat.

Jasmine almost smiled at the diversion.

Almost. All she wanted to do was sleep, but her condo was trashed and she had two state troopers and two trained canines in her space. While she wanted to go to her room, shut the door and pretend none of this was happening, she couldn't. "Now what?"

Again, Will looked at Sean. There seemed to be a brief, silent conversation between the two of them. They'd probably worked together so long that each knew what the other was thinking.

With a brief nod, Will reached for Jasmine's hand and led her to the couch. He set the cushions back into place then gestured for her to sit down.

This was not going to be a good conversation. Her gut and his expression confirmed it. She wanted to argue that she wasn't going to sit, wasn't even sure she *could* sit with all of the adrenaline racing in her veins, but the truth remained that she was too exhausted to fight.

She sank to the sofa, and he settled beside her, closer this time than at the airfield when they'd first met.

She was okay with that. Something in her needed him to be her friend, not just an investigator.

At the door, Sean stood as still as a guard at the queen's palace, but his eyebrow lifted in interest as he watched the two of them.

Jasmine ignored the question on his face, the one Will either didn't notice or didn't care to acknowledge.

With a deep breath, he lifted her hand, staring at it as he traced the knuckle of her index finger. "You can't stay here."

Gently, she extracted her fingers from his grasp and gripped her knees. "It's my home. It's my…" She shook her head. Her voice was weak. She was too tired to argue. Weariness lay on her like a damp wool blanket. Every thought struggled to swim up from the bottom of the ocean.

She knew this feeling, this detached-from-reality feeling. It was anxiety bordering on panic. If she didn't do something soon—get up, get moving, get *out*—she would be staring in the face of a full-blown panic attack marked by the irrational need to run.

Because she'd once actually had to run.

Shoving to her feet, she paced the room, shaking her hands at her sides. The last thing she needed was to blow to pieces in front of Will and his teammate, but there was nowhere to hide. Trying to regulate her breathing, she walked to the short hallway that led past the kitchen to the bedrooms. "I need a minute."

Behind her, the sound of fabric rustling told her Will had stood. "We can't leave you alone."

Jasmine held up her hand and stared at her bedroom door, which hung open. Clothes and bedsheets littered the floor.

It didn't matter what he said. She couldn't do this anymore. "I don't care."

"You should." Will's voice shifted from friend to officer, and it held an edge. "Your home is a crime scene. You can't be wandering around in here until our CSIs sweep it." He stepped closer and rested his hand on her shoulder. "I want to catch who did this, Jasmine. More than you know. But if you want to apprehend these drug runners and protect the people in the villages you're flying to, then you have to walk away now." He gave her shoulder a brief squeeze and lowered his voice. "Pray."

Something in his words knocked the panic down a notch. She pulled in a deep breath. This wasn't about her. From the outside, it appeared to be, but the truth was so much deeper. This was about everyone those money-hungry drug pushers were using and abusing.

This was about a much bigger picture.

"Okay." Will was right. She had to buck up. To find her strength in the God she trusted.

Her life had ceased to be her own the day she became a Christian. And she'd ceased to be herself the day she chose to testify against Anton Rogers.

Yasmine Carlisle was already dead.

She wouldn't let Jasmine Jefferson die, too.

"She knows something." Sean crossed the small hotel room and checked the door between their room and the one they'd secured for Jasmine.

Will's head jerked up from where he was pouring food into Scout's bowl while the collie did a happy dance at his feet. "What do you mean by that?" Was his teammate accusing Jasmine of withholding evidence? Working for the bad guys? Or what?

He ignored the fact that, for a split second when Scout had alerted in Jasmine's living room, he'd wondered if she might be guilty after all. It wouldn't be the first time he'd let a woman dupe him. But the K-9's failure to alert at her presence, her plane or her car said the culprit was a faceless intruder and not her.

Besides, he wasn't in love with Jasmine Jefferson the way he had been with Beth.

With an arched eyebrow, Sean pressed his hand, palm-side down, toward the floor. "Bring it down a notch. I'm not accusing her of anything." His teammate grabbed his backpack off the bed and withdrew a bag of food and a bowl. He filled it and set it on the floor beside the bed he'd claimed then grabbed a second bowl, which he filled with water in the bathroom and set it beside the first.

Grace dug in.

Sean settled onto the edge of the bed and eyed Will. "All I'm saying is, if someone is this determined to come at her, Jasmine knows something. The question is, does she *know* what she knows?"

"Really? You're going to talk in riddles?" Normally, his sense of humor showed up in the bleak moments. It was a known fact among law enforcement, emergency workers and the military that humor was the only way to survive the darkness. Sometimes that humor was dark itself. But this time, Will couldn't find it in himself to joke back.

"So it's finally happened." The knowing tone of Sean's voice raked across Will's last nerve.

"What's happened?"

"A woman managed to get your attention."

Will laughed, but it sounded fake and harsh. He stood and grabbed Scout's water bowl, even though it was still full, and walked into the bathroom. "You're barking up the wrong tree."

"Now who's cracking jokes?"

Walking back into the room, Will paused at Jasmine's door. From the other side, the sound of the TV drowned out any other noise. She'd said something about grabbing a shower and a nap, so it was doubtful she could hear their conversation.

As Scout gave him a puzzled head tilt, he set the bowl down, scratched the collie behind the ears, then dropped into a chair at the table in the corner. "Nobody's got my attention."

"So you usually hold hands with witnesses?"

"I didn't hold her hand." But even as he said it, he remembered. Multiple times in her condo, he'd reached for her, touched her… And yes, held her hand.

Will dropped his head against the wall. There was no sense in arguing. Sean had eyes. "What of it?"

"It was simply an observation."

He glanced at the door again. "I guess when you're forced to stay up looking for bears and fighting off assailants in a busted plane in the middle of nowhere, you get to be friends."

"Kind of like this job makes us a family? Because it's dangerous and a little chaotic?"

"A *little*?" Will picked up a pen that lay on the table and began to tap it on the fake wood, trying to bring his thoughts into some sort of order. "It's out of control right now. In addition to the dozens of usual cases we're investigating, we've got an unofficial case with the Kapowskis and the reindeer ranch. A missing bride who was framed for murder by her killer fiancé and his best man. Oh, and we're trying to find Eli's godmother's family, who are doing their best to stay hidden. I think *chaos* would be easier."

"Speaking of Eli…"

"Last time I talked to him, he was headed to see his godmother. Hospice was a possibility."

"We had a team video conference last night while you were camping." Sean ducked sideways to dodge the pen Will threw. He chuckled, then sobered. "She's not doing well. They did move her into hospice care. Time's running out."

"And we're no closer to finding her family." Will exhaled loudly. "I told him I'd focus some more on that as soon as I wrap this case up and we put this smuggler away."

"We all said the same. The team's committed to finding her son and his family, no matter where he's hiding."

Bettina Seaver's son, Phillip—a committed survivalist—had disappeared into the wilderness outside Anchorage with his family. Locating him was proving to be tougher than some of their actual criminal cases. "When a man doesn't want to be found, there are plenty of ways to stay hidden."

Sean nodded. "And our missing groom and best man are a case in point. But you were talking about your smuggler. Any thoughts there?"

Pointing three fingers in a silent command for Scout to lay on his bed, Will stood and walked to the window. He peeked through the curtains at the nearly empty parking lot, then let the fabric fall. He shouldn't risk being spotted, although he seriously doubted they'd been followed.

Still, two state trooper K-9 SUVs in one place were tough to hide from anyone who knew Jasmine was with them. They'd parked in the back but, if someone was searching, it would only be a matter of time. He swished the curtain with his index finger, then stared at the thin line of light that etched the ceiling from the window. "You want facts or my gut?"

"I know the facts. Let's hear what your gut has to say. It's usually a pretty good indicator of where to go next."

Will grinned. It might sound strange to anyone on the outside, but "gut instinct" was a real thing. It was born out of training and listening to their subconscious minds. The little details in the "back rooms" of their brains were often the ones that yielded the best clues.

Then again, sometimes they were wrong. "So, I'm not a fan of Jasmine's boss, Keith Hawkins. Something about him didn't sit right with me."

"Same." When Will turned, Sean was lying with his hands laced behind his head, staring at the ceiling. "What's bugging you could be the way he was more worried about his damaged planes than he was about the woman who was piloting them."

"Could be." That had definitely rubbed Will the wrong way.

"Okay, but let me play the opposite side. He did see the planes before he saw her. Maybe he's one of those guys who can only deal with one thing at a time, and he prioritizes what's right in front of him."

"Could be. But it also could have been an act. He seemed a little too smooth."

"Are you saying that because of your gut or because of the girl?"

Will's shoulders stiffened. "What does that mean?"

Sean simply shrugged. "Let's follow the trail with this Keith guy and see where we end up. He operates an air freight service with his brother, so he has the perfect setup for running drugs into the bush."

"That's one strike." Will dropped into the chair by the window and stretched his legs out, studying the toes of his boots. He'd have to polish them tonight if he was going to wear them tomorrow. And he still needed a shower, but all of that could wait. "So let's think about why he would put Jasmine in the crosshairs with a false tip. It brings us sniffing close to his operation if he's involved." He glanced at Scout and smiled. "No pun intended."

"That was bad." Sean chuckled but kept his focus on the ceiling. "However, if he didn't have any drugs on the premises at the moment and he knew Jasmine's plane was clean, then what better way to throw suspicion off himself than to call in a fake tip on one of his pilots?"

"And based on build, neither of the brothers was the one who attacked me last night. Which means we have nothing to go on except my gut." Will groaned and, when he did, his stomach growled. "My very *hungry* gut. I haven't had a decent meal in two days, and we missed lunch. Although I did have an amazing home-made ham biscuit this morning."

His breakfast seemed like it had been days ago. He sat up in the chair and dragged his hand down his face, realizing he also needed to shave. It was early evening on a day that had technically begun the day before, and he was ready to feel human again. "Let's get some dinner sent here for us and for Jasmine. Then after I get cleaned up we can go talk to her."

"Sounds like a plan." Sean sat up and pulled his phone from its holster at his hip. "It's possible she's seen something suspicious and doesn't even recognize it. We have to question her."

Jasmine wouldn't like it, not as close as she held her personal life to her vest. But Will had to know everything about her if he was going to save her from a smuggler who was intent on silencing her.

TEN

Fluffing her hair with her fingers, Jasmine crossed the small room and dropped into a chair at a small table. With the curtains closed and the lights on, the room swam in a half darkness that felt more like night than day.

She stared at the TV, not really seeing the people on the screen. Her laptop and some books were in her backpack, but a dull headache driven by stress and lack of sleep made the prospect of either feel like unnecessary torture.

Her stomach tightened and a shudder ran through her. Jasmine pulled her knees to her chest and planted her feet in the chair, wrapping her arms around her legs. This was all too familiar. The sudden flight… The out-of-the-way motel. She'd done this before and had spent too many nights praying she'd never have to do it again.

It was times like these when she missed her mom the most. Always her confidant, always the one with the quiet words to calm Jasmine's heart. The one who had led her to Jesus.

Jesus. Why hadn't she at least thought to grab her Bible?

A Bible.

Jumping up from the chair, she headed for the night-stand between the beds, praying all the way. She eased open the drawer with her bottom lip between her teeth and…

Yes! A blue hard-backed Bible rested in the drawer. With a quick *thank you*, she pulled it out and sat cross-legged on the bed, heading for the verse that had gotten her through the last time she'd had to run for her life. She flipped to the fifth chapter of Hebrews and let her finger skim to verses five and six, where she'd camped for so many months. Even though she could recite it by heart, there was something about reading the printed words that solidified the truth inside her. *I will never leave thee, nor forsake thee. So that we may boldly say, The Lord is my helper, and I will not fear what man shall do unto me.*

There was nothing any man could do to her. Breathing in the peace of that truth, she thumbed over to Psalm 18, the one Deputy Marshal Maldonado had suggested on the night she walked away from her life as Yasmine Carlisle forever. He'd called it the "not My baby" psalm, because God came to the rescue of His child, angry at those who came against His own.

Jasmine shut her eyes. Even now, God saw her. Even now, God protected her. Even now—

Three taps on the interior door pulled her eyes open.

"Jasmine?" Her name came quietly, followed by another tap. "Can I come in?" Will's voice filtered through the door softly, as though he was afraid he'd wake her up if she'd actually taken the nap she'd threatened to take.

Laying the Bible aside, she slid to the end of the bed,

planted her feet on the floor and dragged her fingers through her still-damp hair. "Come in."

Will eased the door open and peeked around it. "Got time to talk for a minute?"

"Sure."

He stepped into the room and left the adjoining door open. He glanced around, then grabbed a chair from the small table and dragged it over, sitting almost knee to knee with her. Glancing behind her, he tilted his head. "You were reading the Bible?"

"And praying."

"Didn't you pray this morning?"

She drew her eyebrows together. "I pray whenever I need to."

"My day's too full and moves too fast to pray all the time."

"That's exactly why I have to pray whenever I need Him." She pulled at a loose thread on the bedspread. While God was a huge part of her life, she wasn't used to talking about Him quite so openly.

"And that's why I make sure to never miss my morning devotion."

"Your devotion? Or your prayers? Because those are two different things. One is learning and listening. One is communicating with—"

Will held his hand up. "Are you about to question my relationship with Jesus?" The words sounded like he was trying to be lighthearted, but something in his eyes was hard.

"You're right. I'm sorry. That's personal, between you and Him." Even though his regimented schedule sounded more like work than a relationship. "I'm just saying you need both in your life. Prayer and—"

"I had a couple of questions, if that's okay."

Jasmine nodded. He clearly didn't want to talk about it. And as she analyzed her words and realized how harsh and judgmental they sounded, she probably wouldn't want to talk to her either. "You can ask me whatever if it will get me home again."

For the first time, she took a good look at him. He'd showered and exchanged his uniform for jeans and a gray long-sleeved T-shirt. He smelled like soap and shampoo. She couldn't deny that he looked very different in "civilian" clothes. The whole picture humanized him even more. Will was no longer the state trooper fighting to stop the drug trade. He was also the guy who knew more about her real life than anyone else, the fierce protector who had inexplicably managed to become her friend.

Since she hadn't looked twice at a man since her new life began over two years earlier, the feeling was too weird to process.

"Jasmine?"

She shook her head, bringing herself back into the present. "I'm sorry. I zoned out on you."

He looked over his shoulder at the other room before turning to her. "Sean's ordering food as soon as he gets out of the shower. You have a preference?"

"Not pizza." She needed a real meal. And the way her stomach tensed, pizza wouldn't help anything.

"I was thinking a burger."

"You seem the burger type."

He arched an eyebrow and smiled. "You think you know me?"

Actually, she did, which was kind of scary. "Maybe. But how about The Cookie Jar? They deliver, and I could go for their country fried steak with mashed potatoes and gravy. They have burgers, too."

"Changed my mind about the burger." He pulled his phone from his back pocket and texted something, then leaned forward and shoved the phone back into his pocket.

That move definitely put him in her personal space for the split second it took him to pocket the device.

She tried not to notice and shifted her focus to the real issue. The tranquility she'd felt only moments before shattered. "I think my identity's been compromised." Tears stung her eyes, and it hurt her entire body to say it. The ache came from deep inside her heart and radiated outward. "I don't want to disappear again." She pushed up and walked to the window, staring at the beige curtains, not daring to peek outside.

"I don't think so." Will's voice was low and soft, almost as peaceful as the words she'd read earlier.

But not nearly peaceful enough.

"Jasmine, I've been in touch with Deputy Marshal Maldonado several times, including ten minutes ago. There's nothing to indicate you've been found. He's had extra eyes put on Anton Rogers in prison. The man hasn't talked to a soul since long before you started working with me."

"What about before?" She spun on her heel and walked toward him, stopping a few feet away. He had to understand how terrified she was. "What if—"

Standing, Will closed the space between them and lightly grasped her upper arms. "Look at me." When she lifted her chin, he dipped his so he could meet her eye. "I'm going to keep you safe."

"How?" The single word was weak and whiny. She hated the sound.

"I will." His eyes searched hers, looking deep as though he could force her to believe him. "Trust me."

But she couldn't. Something inside drove her to flight. Holding up her hands, she backed away. Her heart skittered and fear coursed through her in a way she hadn't felt since she'd first agreed to testify. It tingled in her skin and raced through her veins. "I can't." She was headed straight into a panic attack. "Why is this all so hard now?" It wasn't about the shooting or the plane or her apartment. It was something bubbling to the surface, something she couldn't fight.

Will grabbed her hands. "Breathe in. Take a big, deep breath and hold it."

She tugged, but he didn't let go.

"You can do this. Big breath. Hold it while I count. You ready?" His words were low and soothing. "Come on. In…"

Fighting the instinct to break free, Jasmine drew in a shaky breath and held it while Will slowly counted down from four.

"Breathe out while I count." Once again, he counted from four to one. "Now in."

It might have been his calm voice. The measured breathing. Or it might have been the desperate prayers her brain heaved toward heaven. Whatever it was, her emotions slowed down until she no longer felt like fleeing into the woods was her only option.

Will squeezed her fingers. "Better now?"

"Where did you learn that?"

"Believe it or not, in the army." He gave her hands one more squeeze then released them.

Jasmine waited for him to elaborate. When he didn't, she breathed in another slow breath. "Thank you."

"I think I know why it's bothering you now." Will dragged the chair over to the room's small table and indicated she should sit before he took the one across from her. He clasped his hands on the tabletop. "You're feeling overly emotional because you don't have to keep it inside."

"I don't understand." She'd managed to hold it together for over two years. Falling apart was not an option, especially not when this man and the people on the frontier needed her the most.

"I know your truth, and you finally have an opportunity to be your real self. It's all bubbling to the surface because it can."

She looked up from his fingers to his warm brown eyes, which watched her with an understanding she'd never witnessed before, not even from the therapist she'd worked with in WITSEC. This wasn't just a job for Will. He actually *cared*.

Jasmine drew her lips between her teeth and let him watch her, trying to untangle her thoughts. "Nobody understands what it's like to basically die. I look in the mirror, and I still see Yas—" She bit off the name—*her* name—and started again. "I look in the mirror and I see someone who doesn't exist anymore. There's only Jasmine. Who has no memories. Who has no past. Who is alive but is a made up, fictional person." Sitting back in the chair, she crossed her arms over her stomach. "How do I do this for the rest of my life? It's like being on stage all the time and never being allowed to step out of character to breathe."

Without a word, Will waited. Listened.

"I'm so tired of playing a part. And if Jasmine goes away, too, then I'm so terrified I'll lose myself forever." The words were a harsh whisper, riding the edge of tears she didn't want to shed. She closed her eyes to keep them at bay.

There was a soft rustle, then the chair turned slightly. She opened her eyes to find Will kneeling in front of her, his hands on the arms of the chair. "You will always be you. No matter what your name is or where you live, you will never cease to exist."

"How do you know?"

He brushed a stray hair from her face, tucking it behind her ear, before he rested his palm against her cheek and caught her gaze. "Because I know you."

The air between them charged with something more than comfort.

When he laid his other hand against her cheek, everything else fell away. There was only right now.

There was only Will.

He really did know exactly who Jasmine Jefferson was.

In the moment he talked her down from her panic attack, while his eyes were locked on hers, he'd known. He'd backed away because of the force of that knowing.

But now, kneeling before her with her face cradled in his hands, there was no retreating. There was something about being the one person in her entire everyday world who knew who she really was that reached out and burrowed into his soul. And it made him feel strong. Capable of anything.

Even of trusting someone with his heart again.

She felt it, too, leaning toward him slightly, the expression in her eyes different somehow. She knew—

"So you want a burger? That's what I'm hearing?"

Will dropped his hands from Jasmine's face and broke away so fast, he nearly fell backward. Instead, he scrambled to his feet, shaking his head.

What in the world had he been about to do?

Sean appeared in the doorway staring at his phone screen. "I've always wanted to eat at The Cookie Jar. Saw it on some food channel once." He lifted his head and looked between the two of them. His expression shifted into a question, as though he could feel the charge in the air.

"You watch food TV in your spare time? Maybe we could have you cook dinner instead of ordering out."

Cocking his head like Scout did when he was confused, Sean tried to read Will before he answered. "I watched with Ivy once." Almost as though he regretted bringing the past up, Sean lifted his phone. "I'll have them deliver." He disappeared into the other room, and his voice soon drifted back, placing the order.

"Who's Ivy?" Behind him, Jasmine's voice was low but stronger than it had been before.

"His ex-wife. Pretty sure he regrets the *ex* part, though." It was obvious from the way Sean spoke of Ivy on the rare occasions when he did. A couple of months ago, his teammate had reached out to Ivy for help finding the family of Eli's godmother, but he hadn't spoken much about the interaction. He'd been slightly off his game ever since, though. Not in a major way, but enough that Will had noticed.

"Okay, the food will be here in a little under an hour." Sean came into the room, holstering his phone. He'd also changed into civilian clothes, and it was clear they were all ready to relax for the evening, if they could. "Have you talked to her yet?"

Jasmine stood. "Talked to me about what?"

This really wasn't a conversation he was looking forward to. Will sensed she was the kind of person who didn't offer her trust lightly but, once she did, she would be loyal to the end. He was about to present her with a gut feeling and no evidence to back it up. If he wasn't careful, he could shake her faith in him and in Sean, just when he needed it most.

He glanced at his teammate, who sat on the end of Jasmine's bed.

Will took up a similar seat on the second bed in the room.

Jasmine followed suit, sinking into the chair behind her. Her expression was tight and suspicious, maybe even a little bit fearful. "What's wrong?"

Flight was probably running through her mind again, and Will didn't know a way to stop that. He could reach for her, but Sean was already asking questions about the nature of their relationship and, honestly, Will wasn't sure how to answer them. When it came to Jasmine, his entire world had been rocked.

He focused on the case instead. Bracing his hands beside his hips, he got straight to the point. "What can you tell me about Darrin and Keith Hawkins?"

Jasmine's head jerked as if something flew by her nose. "I'm sorry? Darrin and Keith? My bosses?"

"Yes." Sean leaned forward and rested his elbows on his knees. "We're just trying to cover every angle, to make certain we're looking at all the people who could possibly be involved in smuggling drugs to the frontier. They run an air freight service. That makes them natural suspects."

"There are a lot of air freight services in the area. It could be anyone."

"Humor us." Sean was easygoing, but he was also ready for answers.

Will was glad he'd taken up the pushier role.

With a heavy sigh, she pressed her palm against her forehead and stared at the ceiling as though she was trying to hold a headache at bay. "They're regular guys. Darrin's the friendlier one. Keith's usually pretty quiet, unlike today. They started the company right out of college and have built up a pretty big business. Big enough that I don't think they'd jeopardize it by smuggling anything, and especially not drugs." She shrugged. "I've never seen anything to make me think they're up to something. What makes you suspect them?"

"Like Sean said, the job makes them natural suspects." Will couldn't explain the *why*. Not yet. There was just something about Keith's reactions, about his insistence that Will not fly with Jasmine, that raised red flags. Because if he was so concerned with her safety, he would have been more concerned with bullets flying in her direction than with a man shooting up his plane.

Will sat straighter. *A man shooting up his plane...*

Both Sean and Jasmine seemed to lean closer. She held her hand out then dropped it before she touched him. "You just thought of something. Something not so good for me."

Will turned to Sean. "What exactly did Keith say to you about his plane? In the hallway before you walked into the office?"

Scanning the ceiling as though he could see a replay

there, his teammate lifted one hand slightly from his knee. "He was upset the plane was a mess. Said he had two planes grounded now. Wanted it fixed and wanted to know who would pay for it. Said 'the fool shot...'" Sean's voice trailed off and his eyes snapped down and locked on Will's. "He literally said, 'The fool shot up my plane.'"

That was it! That was the thing that had Will's gut churning. He shot to his feet and walked to the outside door, staring at the fire exit map without seeing it. It wasn't *some* fool or *a* fool. Keith had said *the* fool. "That sounds like familiarity. Like he knows who did it."

"Impossible." Jasmine's voice broke through his thoughts. "First, I've been there two years. I think I'd have noticed anything hinky going on. And second, it can't be true because that would mean..."

There was no need for her to finish the sentence, and she wouldn't with Sean in the room anyway. Because that would mean she'd run straight from the murderous sights of one drug kingpin into the employ of another.

"Is there anything you can think of that Keith or Darrin or anyone at the airfield has done that seems strange. Or out of character?" Sean took over the questions, probably sensing they'd come out more professionally from him. His emotions weren't involved, and it was becoming clearer by the second that Will's definitely were.

She sighed. "We're a family. Once a month when it's nice outside, we have a cookout for lunch. When it's nasty weather, we do potlucks. We take care of each other when somebody's sick. I missed work for a week and a half with some virus and they paid me anyway, even though Keith and Darrin had to take turns flying my routes."

"Flying." Will faced the room again. "Does either Keith or Darrin ever fly?"

"Darrin takes passengers up when we have passenger flights. He enjoys the touristy part, being with people and all. He was with a flight today, which is why he wasn't at the airfield. Keith's more of a numbers and files guy, but he loves to fly. He takes a few of the freight flights each week."

Sean gave him a knowing look. "Any pattern to those flights?"

"I don't know." Jasmine pressed her lips together as she thought. "I've never paid that much attention, to be honest."

"Something feels off." Sean's tone was grim, and Will now knew that this was more than just a *gut* feeling. And if they were right, it could be potentially devastating for Jasmine.

"I'm telling you it's not them, and if you keep looking in their direction you'll miss the real smugglers." Her voice rose and took on a tone he typically often heard when family defended family.

His stomach dropped. She wasn't romantically involved with one of them, was she? If she was, it would be natural to cover for them. He didn't want to ask. Oh, how he didn't want to ask.

But he had to. "Jasmine, are you dating Keith or Darrin?"

Her nose wrinkled as though he'd suggested she lick the carpet. "No."

Sean swallowed a laugh. "Are they that offensive?"

"*What?* No!" She shook off the look and almost

seemed to blush. "They've always treated me like a kid sister, so it's like you asked me if I was dating my brother." The slight amusement seemed to die at the mention of her brother.

She'd left her brother behind when she started her new life, but Sean didn't know that. The air in the room stilled.

Sean looked between the two of them. "Is there something I need to know?"

"No." Jasmine's denial was abrupt, and she stood. "No one at Kesuk Aviation is running drugs."

Sean didn't look convinced, but there was nothing Will could do. Jasmine's WITSEC status had to be guarded, even from his teammate, if she had any chance of keeping her current identity when this was all over.

But what if he was wrong? What if, by keeping that secret, he was putting all of them in even deeper danger?

ELEVEN

Cradling the cup of coffee Will had handed her on the way out of the hotel, Jasmine leaned forward and peered up at the sky through the windshield of his SUV. The early morning sun swiped paintbrush strokes of color along streaks of cirrus clouds. It promised to be a beautiful day for flying, and she wished she could be in the pilot's seat. She itched for the feel of the yoke in her hands and the gentle bobbing of a plane coasting the sky in fair weather.

Up in the air, with the clouds, she felt truly safe. Bullets couldn't reach her there. Faceless assailants couldn't sneak up behind her. No one could tamper with her plane as long as it was in the air.

Then again, someone had managed to get to her plane, but other than a long night in the wilderness, the danger hadn't been too scary. Had she been flying over water, then…

Forget thinking like that. There was enough trouble around her without borrowing more. Cautiously, she took a sip of hot coffee, hoping it would fill in the gaps where her restless sleep had failed to bring restoration. She pulled in a deep breath. It was going to be a *long* day.

"You okay over there?" Will's head turned slightly. Even though he wore sunglasses, it was easy to tell that he was surveilling their surroundings, his vision constantly shifting.

He was watching out for her. She'd hoped never to be in a situation like this again. "Just shaking the feeling of déjà vu. I've been here and done this before." She dared to turn straight toward him. "It did not end well the last time."

The corner of his mouth tipped slightly. "I don't know about that. You're still breathing. I'd say it went pretty well."

"Not if I've been found."

Reaching across the console, Will tapped her hand where it was wrapped around her coffee cup. "I realize you feel like you're facing down your worst-case scenario, but the evidence says you're not. It seems someone thinks you know something, whether you realize it or not. I'm trusting the evidence."

"I thought you trusted your gut."

He chuckled. "My gut's usually working on the evidence my brain doesn't see outright. Subconscious at work."

Well, he might trust his subconscious, but hers was screaming she was on the verge of disappearing. She gripped the fragile coffee cup tighter, then forced herself to loosen her grip before she crushed the thing and made a caffeinated mess of Will's front seat. "I wish I was flying today."

"I know." His voice was gravelly as he slowed to make the turn at the airfield. "It's your safe place."

The understanding of his words rested on Jasmine like a warm blanket on a cold day. It almost felt like she could do anything as long as Will was around.

But he wouldn't be around forever. Either she'd be relocated, or he'd move on to another case. Their days together were numbered.

Days were numbered was a bad choice of words. *Lord, please. Take this fear away.*

"Are you praying?" Will's voice cut her God conversation short.

"Does that bother you?"

He shook his head. "No. It's just different."

"How so?" Jasmine wrinkled her forehead, grateful for the distraction from her thoughts. While she wasn't practiced in talking about God, He was a natural part of the rhythm of her life.

"I guess I never thought about praying all the time. I know there's something in the Bible about praying without ceasing, but you have to live, too. You can't stay in your Bible all day." Overhead, a scattering of ravens broke the cloud-dusted sky.

Jasmine really did wish she was flying. Life was easier in the air. It was also easier when she prayed. "I'm not in my Bible all day. I pray when I need to. God's always there. Maybe if you broke free of your six o'clock appointment, you'd see that." She hadn't meant for the words to be accusatory. "I didn't mean—"

"You didn't mean what? That you know God better than I do?" He didn't seem angry. He sounded almost curious, as though he was coaxing out her thoughts.

"God doesn't want us checking boxes. He wants all of us. All of the time. We live life beside him, not with occasional side trips to him. He's always listening, and I always need Him." She poked her finger into his shoulder. "I promise I'm not judging you. I just see it differently. I guess we all have a unique relationship with Him, or we wouldn't be individuals."

"Maybe." The word came out slowly, but when he hooked a right into the airfield parking lot, he switched topics. "That Ford Expedition. Is that Keith and Darrin?"

"It's Darrin's, but they usually ride together. They don't live far from each other." As Will coasted to a stop in a parking space close to the office building, Jasmine unbuckled her seat belt and watched Sean glide into the space beside them. "I still think it's a waste of time to look at Keith and Darrin. Kesuk Aviation makes good legal money. I've seen the financials. Risking that kind of profit to run drugs would be counterproductive."

"Greed is a strange beast." He switched off the vehicle and faced her, his brown eyes serious. "Do you have any idea what one OxyContin pill can go for in some of the remote villages?"

"No." How could she? "I know the drug problem is rampant in Alaska. Shutting down one supply line won't stop it, not when something like fifteen percent of the population has admitted to using." She flicked the plastic lid on her coffee cup, then wiped away a rogue drop with her thumb. "It's being flown in, snowmobiled in, mailed in… It's so big."

"It is. But shutting down one line can lead to others. We can never stop it, but we can slow it down."

This was what Will and Scout did. They tried to dam up a river with a chain-link fence. "It's hard on you, isn't it? Knowing you can't save them all."

He watched Sean climb out of his SUV. "I'd love to

put a stop to the whole trade, but I'll never be able to."
He shook his head and seemed to come back to the present. "I do what I can to save as many as I can."

Because he couldn't save his own mother. Jasmine wanted to take his hand the way he'd taken hers so many times, but she held back. Will didn't need her comfort. He needed her cooperation. "So how much does Oxy go for?"

"Enough to tempt anyone. Opportunism and greed know no bounds. Neither does evil." He shoved open his door and looked over his shoulder at her as he stepped from the vehicle. "Outside of Alaska, you can pick up a pill for about ten bucks. On the frontier where the supply is thin, and the routes are iffy? We've had reports of one pill going for four hundred dollars." The truck rocked as he shut the door behind him.

Jasmine sank into the seat and stared unseeing out the windshield. Four hundred dollars for *one* pill? A legal thirty-day prescription could go for twelve thousand dollars. Someone could buy hundreds of pills in the lower forty-eight and transport them here for a profit that tested her math skills.

And that was just one drug. There were dozens of others that likely brought big money as well.

She covered her mouth and let her chin fall toward her chest. Not only were people's lives in danger, but their livelihoods were as well if they were willing to pay that much for a momentary high. The villages weren't prosperous places. Most folks scraped to get by. So many had children. She knew from experience with some of her former students that, when addiction struck, parents would neglect their families to get the fix they needed, even to the point of homelessness.

Or *worse.*

These perpetrators were taking advantage of people in order to get rich. They were trashing the lives of people on the frontier who were simply trying to survive in a land that was already stacked against them.

She was in Alaska because of men like that. She'd actively participated in taking one of their killers down at a cost almost too high to bear. *Lord, forgive me for being afraid. For forgetting I gave my life to You to do with as You wish. You didn't bring me to Alaska for no reason. You saw all of this coming from the moment I was born. You put me here to help. You brought Will in because You knew I could do more if I joined him in this investigation. So I will.*

I will.

Something about Jasmine had changed.

As he held the door to Kesuk Aviation open and ushered her inside, he could feel it in the tilt of her head and the straightness of her spine.

There was no doubt where this strength had come from. He'd seen the same behavior in soldiers and law enforcement officers he'd worked with over the years. He'd felt it in himself. It was the thing that drove him.

Jasmine was a warrior. When Will had informed her how lucrative the illegal drug trade was, that fierce valor had kicked into high gear. She saw what he saw… lives wrecked not only emotionally and physically, but financially as well.

There was no doubt she was done being afraid. She was ready to fight.

When the door closed behind him, he shifted his thoughts to the mission. What she'd said about God and prayer resonated, but he'd always been that guy who spent time in prayer first thing in the morning, waited for his marching orders, and went on with his day.

Was it possible God wanted more?

In the hall, Jasmine eyed him with a silent question.

He nearly smiled. That was one brave, selfless woman. He wouldn't mind being partnered with her for the rest of his life.

His toe caught on the heavy mat inside the door, and he stumbled. *The rest of his life?*

Absolutely not. The last time he'd trusted his heart to a woman, she'd crushed his emotions and nearly derailed his career. He wasn't making that mistake again.

Even if Jasmine didn't seem the type to play that game.

Yeah, he hadn't thought his mother or Beth was capable of that either.

"Are you with us, Will?" Sean stepped up on his heel and kept his voice low.

His teammate was right. He couldn't afford to walk into this situation, where they were trying to figure out if Keith and Darrin were involved, without his mind fully engaged. If Keith's words yesterday were aimed at the shooter, then this was a dangerous game, and he couldn't afford to take his eye off the ball.

The cost might not be his life.

It might be Jasmine's.

She'd stopped at the door to a small break room. "What are we doing?"

"Not much." Will kept his voice low. "Without a warrant, we can't search. I want to ask your bosses some follow-up questions, see if they slip up. You can give us a tour of the building, but I'd like to get a look around the hangars. It's a gray area, but if I'm out there at your invitation and Scout happens to alert, then we're on safe legal ground."

Jasmine's eyes slipped shut, but she nodded. She obviously still wasn't on board with his theory, even though Keith's comment had been chilling.

"Who's flying today?" Sean stepped up next to Will, and Grace sat at his heel.

"I'm off today. I think Keith is taking a run up to Windward Fort. He typically takes off around eight." She glanced at her watch. "It's a little after seven now."

"Jasmine." A voice from up the hall drew all of their attention. A slim man in his early thirties with dark hair and blue eyes stepped closer. "What are you doing here?" He glanced at his phone and thumbed through a few screens, then typed something. "I don't have you on the schedule for today." When he lifted his head, he eyed Will and Sean with a wariness that was either suspicion or concern.

Jasmine gave a small wave. "Darrin, this is Trooper Will Stryker and Trooper Sean West." She gestured back toward the man. "This is Darrin Hawkins, the co-owner of Kesuk Aviation."

Darrin hesitated, then stepped forward and shook both Will's and Sean's hands. "I'm sorry we have to meet under such circumstances. I was on a flight yesterday and missed the excitement here. I hear you're going to continue to fly with Jasmine, Trooper Stryker? We'll help in any way we can to stop the flow of drugs to the frontier."

"That's not what your brother said." Will's voice held a slight edge. If he kept Darrin off balance, he might slip the way his brother had.

"Keith can be overly cautious, and he's concerned about Jasmine." The answer was even and polished.

Almost *too* polished. "Yesterday he seemed more concerned about the damage to his planes."

Darrin smiled softly. "That sounds like Keith. He's the numbers and the brains here. Without him, we'd have folded on year one." His gaze never broke from Will's.

The hairs on the back of Will's neck bristled. From experience, that kind of forced, direct gaze usually indicated someone was hiding something and didn't want to *look* like they were hiding something. It wasn't natural. "And what do you do around here?"

"I'm the face of the business. The handshaker. The one who brings in new clients and smooths over things with the old ones. Keith's all about numbers. I'm all about people."

That explained the manufactured smoothness that crawled under Will's skin. The guy was a salesman, and he was playing that role with all he had.

There was a standoff as the three men sized one another up while Jasmine watched. Outside, the whine of a plane's engine revved, then passed as it lifted. The sound was loud in the silence.

Darrin looked away first. He glanced at his phone. "I've got a call with a potential new client in Anchorage, so I need to head back to my office. Is there anything I can help you with, Jasmine? Did you need something?"

"I just wanted to check on the planes. That Twin Otter is my baby, you know." She spoke the line just like Will had asked her to. Her delivery was flawless. *Good job, Jas.*

"Jerry's in the hangar with the Twin Otter now. She

should be good to go for you to fly tomorrow. The Piper's going to take longer. Keith is flying the King Air this morning." He addressed Will. "And what's *your* reason for being here?" He glanced at Jasmine with a raised eyebrow as though hinting at something personal between them.

No way was Will taking that bait. "Jasmine was the target of a false tip, sabotage and a shooting. If it's okay with you, we'd like to stay close to her while she's here. We'd also like to look around to see if our evidence team might have missed anything after the shooting."

Darrin shrugged. "Be my guest. Just don't get in anyone's way. With two planes grounded, we're pushing hard to stay on top of things." He moved to step around the men. "Jasmine, you're on the run to Innesreh and Winchinechen tomorrow, right?"

"That's the plan. I haven't looked at the latest schedule, so I'll take your word for it."

"You haven't?" Darrin's head drew back slightly, but then he shrugged and typed something into his phone. "I'll have Christy print you a copy." When he was finished with his phone, he pocketed it. "Guys, it's good to have you out here. I've seen what the drug trade can do to the frontier. Fewer drug supply lines makes things better for everybody." With a nod, he walked away and disappeared around the corner of the short hallway.

Sean and Will both watched him go.

"He rubs me the *wrong* way in a *big* way," Sean muttered.

"Same."

With a loud sigh that said more than words ever could, Jasmine held her hand out to the room at her right. "You wanted a tour? This is the break room. Your 'basic fridge, snack machine, table and chairs kind of place."

Stepping into the doorway, Will dropped Scout's leash and gave a quick command.

The K-9 squeezed past him and sniffed around the room. Near the drink machine, he hesitated then seemed to follow some sort of trail back to Will, but he didn't alert. Instead, he sat at Will's feet and looked up, ready for whatever came next.

And he was certainly disappointed. Scout's training had taught him to associate the scent of narcotics with a favorite toy and a treat. Coming up empty on a search was no fun for his partner. Will gave him a quick pat on the head when he reached down and picked up the leash. It had been a busy and frustrating couple of days. He'd have to make sure Scout got some good playtime this afternoon. A restless border collie was prone to mischief, even one as well trained as Scout.

They proceeded to the T in the hallway. Jasmine pointed in the direction opposite of the way Darrin had gone. At the end of the hall, a heavy door stood sentry. "We'll go that way last. Keith's office is down there, as you know from yesterday. There's a supply closet and a small room we use on the very rare occasion we have a meeting."

Will scanned the area, noting Keith's office door was tightly closed. "You said he's on a flight?"

"He's probably out in the hangar doing final loading and prep." Glancing at her watch, Jasmine led them in the direction Darrin had gone. "We'll catch him before he leaves if we don't take too long in here."

As they walked down the short hallway, Will kept his attention on his surroundings, looking for anything out of place. Behind him, in an unspoken agreement, he knew Sean watched their backs and also surveilled the area.

He tightened his grip on Scout's leash as they passed a closed door that bore Darrin's name. From inside, the man's voice drifted out, but it was impossible to make out any words.

It would be interesting to know who he was really chatting with, because Will was almost certain it had nothing to do with clients in Anchorage. Especially after that one comment, the one about how it would be better for everyone when there were fewer drug supply lines. Not *no* lines, but *fewer* lines. *Fewer* meant more money in the pockets of the ones who managed to escape detection.

Will bit the inside of his mouth. Either Keith and Darrin were both prone to verbal slips, or he had become way more cynical and suspicious than he'd ever wanted to be.

After a quick walk-through of a small waiting area and a brief introduction to a woman named Christy, who manned the radio and generally assisted Keith and Darrin, Jasmine led the way back toward Keith's office and shoved open the outside door.

Unlike the wide glass doors in the waiting area, which led directly out to the runway, this door placed them next to the hangars. It was the same door they'd entered yesterday when the shooting had stopped.

Jasmine led the way, looking over her shoulder as she walked. "This first hangar is where the King Air lives. I don't see it on the runway so Keith must still have it in the hangar. It's about an hour before he typically takes off, so he might still be loading."

As they walked around the front of the building, she entered the huge hangar doors then stopped suddenly, looking out at the airfield.

Will already knew what she saw. The plane—and Keith—were gone.

The leash in his hand pulled taut.

Will glanced down. Scout strained against his hold, eager to explore the hangar, so he let him go.

His partner sniffed around the floor, then trotted to the center and sat, watching Will with an expectant gaze.

Behind him, Sean muttered something unintelligible, but Will didn't have to understand the words to know what he'd said.

There had been drugs in the hangar. *This morning.*

TWELVE

What was going on? Jasmine stepped into the hangar, part of her hoping she'd somehow missed the plane. The building was small, meant to house only one aircraft, and there was no way it was hiding behind a tool box or a ladder. Other than Scout sitting in the middle of the floor watching Will, there was nothing.

Once again, she walked to the door, shielded her eyes, and scanned the single runway and the rest of the airfield. No sign of the King Air and no sign of Keith.

"He left already?" Will stood beside her, but he wasn't looking at her. His tone and stance said he was more suspicious than ever of the men she considered to be her friends.

But even she couldn't deny the behavior was odd. "I don't see him." She exhaled slowly and thought through the conversation with Darrin. He hadn't indicated his brother would be heading out early. "Keith is one of those people who values his routine. Every flight, barring a weather hold, he takes off at the same time, without fail. It's not like him to break protocol." Her gaze followed Will's, which wasn't on her. It didn't even appear he was listening to a word she said.

Instead, he stared at Scout, who had planted himself in the middle of the hangar watching Will intently, an eager gleam in his eye.

He'd done the exact same thing in her condo. The dog was waiting for a treat, because the scent of drugs meant a reward was on the way.

Her stomach roiled. *No.* Will and Sean couldn't be right. If they were, that meant she was working for the very kind of men who had ruined her life the first time. It meant she couldn't even trust people she'd come to rely on as family. It meant her job, her life and everything she knew was about to evaporate before her eyes, whether her identity was safe or not.

It meant Darrin and Keith were the kind of men who'd hurt others to line their pockets.

"He's wrong." She shook her head slowly from side to side. "Scout has to be wrong."

Will bit down on his lower lip, no doubt holding back an assertion like *Scout is never wrong.*

"Maybe it's not what it looks like." An idea sparked and she walked closer to the trooper, praying he'd hear what she was about to say. "Maybe Keith had a prescription supply to run up today. We don't fly them a lot, but he's the one who takes the cargo when we do. Maybe Scout's alerting to a perfectly legal shipment of medications."

Will glanced at Sean, then dipped his head toward the main hangar door. When the other man led Grace to the opening and stood watching the runway, Will turned to Jasmine. "You and I both know how legal medications are shipped, at least the ones Scout would alert to. They're in sealed containers inside locked boxes typically made of metal. My partner's good at what he does, and it's true he can latch onto residue left behind off someone's clothes, but he can't smell through sealed metal boxes. Even he's not that good." He reached down, scratched Scout behind the ears, and pulled a red rubber chew toy from his bag.

Scout settled down with the treat, happily gnawing away.

The collie made this look like a game, like fun was waiting to happen. This was so much more than that. This was life and death for people living on the frontier. And it was an upending of Jasmine's life once again if things got out of hand. What if she had to testify again? Wouldn't that bring her out into the open? *Lord, I said I'd do anything, but I need You to give me the strength to do it.*

He'd come through in the past. She had to believe He'd come through again.

She straightened her shoulders and prepared for battle. "Okay, let's say you're right. Just for the sake of argument, and not because I think you are. Then it's an easy fix. You treat Keith like you did me. You meet him when he lands at Windward Fort and you sweep the plane. You'll either find something or you won't."

"I wish it was that easy, Jas. But it took twenty-four hours to set up the operation and get into place to board your plane. We had permission from Keith and Darrin to do so, so we didn't need a warrant. This time, if Keith is truly ferrying drugs, I highly doubt they'll clear our path like that again." A muscle twitched in his jaw. "Besides, if they are behind this, I don't want to show them yet that I know. They could shut down for a while and keep us from finding anything, then start back up again when the heat is off them."

"Plus, he's got a good twenty-minute head start on us."

Will narrowed his eyes. "What makes you say that?"

"When we were inside, talking to Darrin, a plane took off. It sounded like it could have been the King Air, but we get a lot of personal planes in and out, too, so I really didn't pay that much attention. However, given that Darrin said Keith was still here and that he's not here now? And also considering that's the only plane I've heard leave?" She didn't want to say it, but she also wouldn't hide the truth. "I'm guessing Keith took off when we arrived."

"Darrin was texting someone when he saw us. Could have been a warning."

"Or it could have been the company in Anchorage that he's courting." She wasn't ready to buy that her bosses were the problem, that they were responsible for a good man like Casey Bell overdosing and having to be flown out of Landsher in a fight for his life. "You know, up until I saw Anton Rogers shoot a man, drug dealers and smugglers were always faceless and nameless. In my mind, all they did was ruin lives and sit around counting their money and building up their arsenals. I never imagined they were the kind of people you might be eating beside in a restaurant or passing in the grocery store aisle." *Or be working for.*

The pain in her stomach nearly doubled her over. There was no way she was working for smugglers. No. Way.

A worse thought whipped through her. "Will." Jasmine's voice came out in a ragged whisper. "What if I've had drugs on my flights before and didn't know it? What if someone loaded a shipment in with my cargo?"

Without a word, Will drew her to him and held her close. She rested her head on his shoulder, feeling the beat of his pulse in his neck. "Jas, you can't live in the hypotheticals. That's my job. If this is true, I don't think they would risk their profits or their freedom with someone who might randomly find their stash. Based on the evidence so far, Keith is probably flying the real drug flights."

This couldn't be true. Her whole world was upside down if it was.

Will's arms tightened around her. "Give me a copy of the flight schedule, and I'll see about gathering enough evidence for a warrant so we can get an operation rolling to board his plane the next time he flies." His words brushed against her hair. "Until then, all we can do is wander. We have consent from Darrin to be here, so if Scout stumbles on something, it's admissible."

He pulled away and cupped her face in his hands. "You're right that all I have right now is essentially circumstantial. I'm going to need more. And I'm going to need your help to unearth it."

With a nod, Jasmine backed away from his touch. Everything about her roiled in conflict, from her stomach to her heart to her head. Will was the closest thing she had to a real friend. The only person who knew who she really was and how deep her suffering ran. He was also the heroic state trooper who was out to protect the men and women on the frontier from the drug dealers who would destroy lives to stuff their bank accounts.

But he was also the man who was accusing the people she cared about, the employers who offered her the livelihood she loved. Everything in her hoped and prayed she was the one who was right.

Will's investigation made him the enemy to her friends and to her comfortable career. She couldn't reconcile that truth with the man who not only truly knew her heart, but who was starting to hold that heart in his hands as well.

She'd lead them on a tour of the rest of the airfield, then she'd visit Jerry and see how the Twin Otter was coming along. In the process, maybe she'd be able to prove that Kesuk Aviation had simply been the victim of a false tip, and that everyone she worked for was who she believed them to be.

"The storage sheds are between the hangars, so Scout can have a sniff at them, but they're locked. We keep cargo under lock and key unless we're loading and unloading. Too many people would love to plunder the kind of stuff we move in and out. They'd make a fortune on the black market. After that, we can check the hangars and stop back by the office to get the flight schedule from Christy."

"Sounds like a plan." Will gave Scout a command, then placed the chew toy back in his backpack. He petted the collie on the head when Scout heeled, then they headed toward the door with his K-9 on the leash between them. "I know this isn't easy for you. Don't think I don't appreciate what you're doing." Will's voice was low, meant for her ears only.

It coated her heart with something warm. Something she really wasn't sure she wanted to feel about him.

"Okay, Sean." Will raised his voice so the other man could hear as they approached him. "Jasmine's going to finish giving us the tour." He stepped into the sunlight.

She walked out with him, shielding her eyes against the morning sun. It might actually be warm enough to—

Three rapid cracks broke the morning stillness.

Fire scorched her shoulder. As Will shoved her deeper into the hangar, Jasmine clutched her shoulder and felt the warm blood.

* * *

"Jasmine's hit!" Will grabbed Jasmine by the arm and dragged her into the back corner of the hangar, away from the angle the shooter had on them.

With his leash dragging, Scout rushed along beside them.

From outside, shouts came from multiple directions, but they were unintelligible past the pounding of adrenaline through Will's system.

Closer to the door, Sean ducked for cover with Grace behind him and eased out to try to survey the area. He held his sidearm at the ready. "You calling it in?"

"Got it." Will settled Jasmine on the floor against the wall. Resting one hand on her bicep, he knelt beside her and jerked his radio from its holster. Then he identified himself and gave his location to dispatch. "Shots fired. Pedestrian struck. Request backup. Dispatch fire/medic to my location. Location of shooter unknown at this time."

From the far end of the runway, tires squealed. "Can you see him?" Hopefully Sean had made out something.

"Black coupe on the other side of the airfield. Can't tell make, model or plate. Too far away."

Will relayed the information to dispatch, then pulled gloves from his belt and drew them on.

Jasmine didn't move or speak. She watched with wide eyes, probably in shock. If the wound wasn't bad, then the suddenness of the attack and the accuracy of the shot had likely muddied her mind.

Scout hovered beside her, then lay down and nudged his nose under her hand where it rested on the concrete.

"It's going to be okay." *God, let it all be okay.* Will threw the prayer at the sky along with a lot of more desperate, unintelligible ones. Easing her jacket away from her shoulder, he surveyed the damage.

"How bad?" Jasmine seemed to come back to him, and her fingers eased gently over Scout's head. His partner was a stellar sniffer, but sometimes he was even better at offering comfort. His presence definitely seemed to be working on Jasmine.

There was a rip in her jacket and in her shirt. He eased the cloth apart. The bullet had grazed her arm just below her shoulder, leaving behind a wicked burn and a rapidly bruising shallow cut.

He exhaled and lowered his head with a quick prayer of gratitude.

"Will?"

Rocking back on his heels, he laid his hand on her forearm and watched her face. "It's superficial. How bad is it hurting?"

"It stings. Nothing awful." She sagged against the metal wall as the sound of sirens grew louder. "How did this happen?"

"You mean how did someone know you'd be here?" He had his suspicions. Darrin could have slipped around to the other side of the airfield. Or maybe Keith wasn't on that plane after all.

"No. How did they not kill me?" Her voice was weak. Her skin was pale, and a fine sweat sheened her forehead.

Will couldn't fault her for the question. Getting shot—even grazed—was nothing to shrug off. "I'm going to have to go with God on that one." The shooter had clearly waited for Jasmine to exit the hangar. If she wasn't the target, he'd have fired at Sean, who was by the door, or at Will, who'd walked out first.

Somehow, the bullet had traveled between her and

Will with minimal damage. If one of them had been standing a couple of inches to either side…

"Backup's here. I waved the paramedics this way." Sean approached, holstering his pistol. "I'm fairly certain that car taking off was our man. Hopefully the description of the car was enough so that they can apprehend him."

Two paramedics rushed in with their equipment. Will gave them a quick rundown, squeezed Jasmine's hand and stepped back, motioning for Scout to stay beside her. She seemed to draw more comfort from the collie than from him.

Will walked a few feet away with Sean, but he kept his eyes on Jasmine. He was half-afraid to look away. Every time he let his guard down, it seemed someone managed to get a potshot in.

His teammate stared out the front of the hangar, where two more troopers entered. "This guy's bold, going after her twice in the same way."

"Or he's comfortable here." As Will spoke, Darrin appeared at the entrance to the hangar. One of the troopers stopped him, and he tried to look around the woman to see Jasmine. "Darrin had time to get into position if he left the building when we did. He's had time to stow a vehicle and get back here, too."

Sean shook his head. "It's not him. Within a minute of the shots, he tried to exit the building. I had to wave him back in. He couldn't have been on the other side of the airfield."

That was either a relief or a blow to his case. The pounding in Will's head as his adrenaline ebbed wouldn't let him puzzle out the answer. "How do we know Keith took off in the plane? He could be on the other end of that weapon."

"He could. But I'd think that would be easy to corroborate with anyone around here. A call directly to the plane from their radios here ought to tell us if he's on board."

"The woman we met earlier… Christy? She should be able to do that." Will tapped his fingers against the flashlight hanging from his belt as he watched the paramedics speak in low tones with Jasmine. "We can have her radio him to let him know what happened, and that should keep him from realizing we're checking up on him. Can you be in there to listen to his response, see if you can gauge anything?"

"On it." Sean walked away, but then he turned back. He eyed Will, then looked at Jasmine. "Be careful, Stryker." With a nod to the paramedics, he headed for the building, speaking to Darrin as he passed, who fell into step beside him.

Be careful. Because of the shooter? Or because he sensed something between Will and Jasmine?

He shook his head. Jasmine had become a friend. Nothing more. She couldn't be anything more. He wasn't going down that road ever again.

"Trooper?" The female paramedic looked over her shoulder from where she crouched on the floor at Jasmine's side.

He stepped over and knelt beside her.

Jasmine reached for his hand, slight desperation in her gaze. "I'm not going to the hospital."

"She's refusing transport." The male paramedic looked up at Will with a *Help us with this stubborn woman* plea in the arch of his eyebrow.

"Will, please." Her voice was tinged with an emotion he couldn't place. She ought to be checked out, just to be sure, even though he was certain the injury was minor. Why wouldn't she want to play it safe and have a doctor—

"Oh." He rocked back on his heels as understanding crept in. Everything she did opened her up to discovery. Even small things could have huge ramifications if her photo somehow floated out to the wrong people. Jasmine was still fairly new to witness protection. She still guarded her identity with obsessive attention and wouldn't go anywhere that might put her on the radar any more than she had to.

Tears pooled at the corner of her eyes, and Will had the mad urge to pull her close, but he refrained. Right now, it was enough that she knew he understood.

"How bad is it?" He addressed the female paramedic. "Are we talking stitches?"

"It's superficial. At minimum, keeping it covered should help. So will some ibuprofen and lots of it when her adrenaline wears off and it starts throbbing. At worst, antibiotics wouldn't be a bad idea. We recommend any gunshot victim be transported, though."

Jasmine shook her head, her eyes wide.

Her fear tore at his heart. "Have her sign a refusal of transport. She's in my protection. If she needs to go later, I'll take her."

Neither of the paramedics appeared to like his answer, but Jasmine was his biggest concern. Three times while she was in his care, someone had managed to reach her. And each time, the danger had drawn closer.

The next time might be the time the bullet found its mark.

THIRTEEN

A squeaking, out-of-control squeal jerked Will out of sleep. A mournful dog howl overlapped the din.

Sitting straight up, Will fumbled for his weapon, squinting in the sudden brightness. Not at his hip. Where was he?

Grimacing against the noise, which stopped abruptly, he fought for full alertness. The airport. Jasmine was shot and refused transport. They ushered her back to the hotel.

The hotel.

Will squeezed his eyes tight and opened them slowly against the light, shaking his head to clear it. The beige pattern on the bedspread hurt his eyes. He must have been sleeping hard. Scrubbing the cobwebs away with the palms of his hands, he glanced in the direction of the hideous screech.

Sean sat on the edge of his bed, harmonica in hand.

Will swung his legs around and dropped his feet to the floor. He pressed his palm to his forehead, hoping to stem the dull ache building in his brain. "Seriously?"

With a grin, Sean blew a quick, discordant note, and Grace yipped a high-pitched bark. "Yes, *seriously.* I have to practice, and Grace likes to sing along."

"In a hotel? Where we're trying to lie low and people are probably trying to sleep?" Will tried to see the clock, but it faced the other man. "What time is it?"

"Not time for anybody to sleep." Sean blew three quick notes that had not a single thing to do with one another, then wiped down the harmonica and laid it on the nightstand. "It's not quite three in the afternoon. I convinced you that you needed to rest since you didn't sleep last night and told you I'd keep watch. You racked out when we got back here. Remember any of that?"

"Vaguely." Will scratched his cheek and glanced at the door between the two hotel rooms. It was cracked open slightly. "How's Jasmine?"

"Asleep when I checked ten minutes ago."

"Even with the racket you were causing?"

"Not racket. Music."

Will arched an eyebrow as he stood and headed for the door. He wanted to see for himself that nothing had happened to Jasmine while he was resting. He hated being out of commission but, for the safety of them all, downtime was necessary. "If that was music, what song was it?"

"'Twinkle, Twinkle, Little Star.'"

"No." There was no way that noise was a beloved childhood classic. He pulled the door open gently and peeked into the room.

Jasmine lay on her side with her knees bent. Her breathing was even. Either she was even more exhausted than he was or she had the ability to sleep through the mournful death wail of a suffering water buffalo.

"I can play it again."

"Please, no." His head couldn't take it.

Neither could his stomach. He was starving. "We

have anything to eat?" There were some protein bars in his backpack, but that wasn't going to cut it.

Sean pointed at the corner. "There are subs in the mini fridge. I had some delivered while you were snoring."

"I don't snore." Will glanced at Scout, who was content on his bed, then checked to make sure there was water in the bowl. Grabbing a sub, he dropped into a chair at the table and was halfway through the sandwich before he felt awake. "Thanks."

"No problem." Sean glanced at his watch. "I woke you up on purpose. We've got a video teleconference with the team at three. You have about two minutes to shove that sandwich down your throat and make your bed head look presentable."

Will balled up his napkin and threw it at Sean, then grew serious. "Any idea why? A VTC in the middle of the day when most of us are on assignment means something's up."

"No idea. Eli's text just said it was an all-hands and to be sure we were available." Sean pulled his laptop from his backpack and positioned it on the table between them. "You got a text, too, I'm sure."

Swallowing the last bite of ham and turkey, Will pulled his phone from its holster. Yep.

There was a also a text from Deputy Marshal Maldonado, stating that, while Jasmine's identity hadn't been compromised, there was something more happening with Anton Rogers. He was following up on it but didn't think it had anything to do with Jasmine.

That was a relief. He couldn't bear to see her life ripped apart again.

Another text, this one from fellow trooper Helena

Maddox, reminded him how quick he was to believe in guilt over innocence. She must have been talking to Sean.

Well, he had news for the two of them. His thought process was slowly changing. He'd been wrong about Jasmine.

Could he be wrong about Darrin and Keith as well? Sean had seen Darrin in the building during the shooting. Keith had responded on the radio, and GPS had placed his plane over the frontier.

He needed to sit down with Sean and go over facts, not feelings. Somewhere, they were missing something.

Will gripped the phone tighter. He'd respond to Helena later. Right now, he felt like this case had blown into a thousand questions, and his brain couldn't form a coherent picture.

While Sean dialed into the VTC, Will drained a bottle of water and dragged his hands over his hair. He hated the way he felt when he slept in his uniform. It was hot and uncomfortable and, even though he was pretty sure he'd been flat on his back, he felt rumpled and wrinkled.

While he preferred jeans and sweatshirts to his buttoned-down uniform, he took pride in being polished and professional. Right now, there wasn't time to change.

"Will." Sean waved his attention toward the screen with two fingers. "We're starting."

Sliding closer, he surveyed the screen. His teammates were scattered around the state, working cases that called for the expertise of their specialized K-9 unit. Their faces filled multiple windows on the laptop. Poppy Walsh seemed to be at home on her couch with her Irish wolfhound, Stormy. Hunter McCord and Maya Rodriguez both appeared to be in offices, though neither of the spaces looked familiar. The rest of the team was assembled as well, with Colonel Lorenza Gallo and Trooper Gabriel Runyon sharing a screen in her office. Both of them looked troubled.

Will and Sean glanced at each other as the colonel opened the meeting. She seemed to look straight through the screen at each of them individually. "We'll start with the quick and easy. Will?"

"Yes?"

"Just before we came online, we got word of another anonymous tip on your drug investigation that came in early this morning, but it got lost in the shuffle of bigger news. Flight out of Kodiak about two hours ago. It's too late to move on it, but I'll text you the details. I want you or Sean to follow up."

A tip for this morning leaving an airport three flight hours away. Likely, it was as dead in the water as the other leads had been. "One of us will look into it."

The colonel gave a curt nod, then handed the meeting over to Gabriel. Whatever was happening, this was the meat of the call. Unexplained dread drove through Will.

Gabriel faced the camera, his blue eyes dark. "We've had a break in the Missing Bride case, although I wish we hadn't. Not this way."

Somebody was dead.

Will scanned the screen to make sure his entire team was present. Only a slight bit of tension released from his chest when he finished his perusal with all accounted for. They might all be safe, but somewhere, another trooper or a civilian was likely not so fortunate.

It had been five long months since the tour guide

for Violet James's wedding party was murdered. Five months since someone shoved bridesmaid Ariel Potter off a ledge while she was taking a photograph. She had survived and was now engaged to Trooper Hunter McCord.

Initially, the team had suspected Violet James was the killer since she'd been implicated by the groom, Lance Wells, and his best man, Jared Dennis. She'd vanished without defending herself.

However, Wells and Dennis were now on the run, and new evidence had surfaced implicating them as the killers, while Violet's life was still in danger. Other than random sightings in and around Anchorage, there had been no confirmed evidence of where Violet James, Lance Wells or Jared Dennis had disappeared to.

Gabriel spoke again, his tone grave. "There was a home invasion in Anchorage last night. Jewelry, credit cards and approximately seven hundred dollars in cash were taken from the home and its owners." He glanced at something on the desk in front of him. "A thirty-eight-year-old male, air force senior master sergeant James Alessandro, and his wife, a thirty-six-year-old woman named Elsa Alessandro were killed."

Brayden Ford frowned from his box on the screen. "I'm guessing since this is tied to the Missing Bride case, that our suspects are Lance Wells and Jared Dennis?"

The team looked stricken. Death, especially death at the hands of suspects they had yet to apprehend, was especially hard.

The team's forensic scientist, Tala Ekho, waved a hand. "Fingerprints from the scene point to both men being present. Further, Jared Dennis got sloppy. He drank out of an orange juice container while they were in the house. DNA from the container is conclusive." She scanned the tablet she held. "Elsa Alessandro was shot in the back of the head and died instantly. The master sergeant was shot in the chest and died in surgery, but he was able to give a statement before he passed. He told troopers on the scene that the men in his house were the men from the news who were wanted for the murder in Chugach."

Confirmation that Wells and Dennis were cold-blooded killers. The victory was unbelievably hollow. Two innocent people were dead, randomly attacked by men who cared only for themselves.

"They're desperate if they're willing to move into the open and brazenly kill." Colonel Gallo's voice was hard. There was no doubt she felt some responsibility for the murders. They all did. "The situation is escalating. We have to find the men and Violet James as soon as possible, before more people die. I have no doubt they're searching for Violet, or they wouldn't risk staying in that area. We've had unconfirmed reports of her being spotted around Anchorage, so it's only a matter of time before they find her or kill someone else."

Will drummed his fingers on the table. The team had to prevent more deaths. They had to bring Wells and Dennis to justice and to save Violet James. "I wish we could find a way to reach her, to let her know we can protect her. Given that she was not only a suspect but a target of the killers, she may never show her face again."

"Sean." The colonel focused on the camera. "Can you reach out to Ivy again? See if she's been able to find anything?"

Beside Will, Sean tensed. There was a very uneasy

truce between Sean and his ex-wife, who ran a Christian mission that offered aid and supplies to survivalists near Nome. They suspected Violet was hiding with someone in the wilderness, but survivalists were notoriously closemouthed. Gathering information was tough. "Ivy came up empty last time, but I can try."

There was something behind Sean's words and posture that said reaching out to his ex hurt more than he wanted to admit. He'd been struggling since their last contact.

Will would have to ask him about it later.

"We'll touch base again when DNA evidence comes back." The colonel was closing the VTC. "Until then, keep your eyes open. And be safe." She shut down the call, and the screen went dark.

Will sat back in his chair. "So we have proof that Lance Wells and Jared Dennis are in Anchorage and are capable of murder."

"I know those names." From behind them, Jasmine's voice floated over the room.

Will jumped to his feet to find Jasmine standing in the doorway, her shirt wrinkled and her face bearing the imprint of the pillow on her cheek. She wasn't supposed to be in on a secure meeting.

What else had she heard?

"Was that about Violet James?" Jasmine stepped farther into the room as Sean and Will cast sideways glances at one another.

Oh, no. She probably wasn't supposed to hear what was said in their video conference call. But some tortured wailing noise had pulled her out of sleep, and she'd heard voices, so she'd stepped in to investigate.

Being alone, even with Sean and Will in the next room, wasn't something she was fond of at the moment, not when it felt as though someone was watching her every move.

She was also hungry. The kind of hunger that came from crashing adrenaline and too much stress. Other people couldn't eat when they were worried. She plowed through chips and salsa like the salty crunch was key to survival.

Sean closed the laptop and pushed it toward the wall. "She's going to see it on the news anyway. Once this hits, it's going to be big."

So it *was* about the murder investigation that the news had dubbed the "Missing Bride" case. The media had a field day with the oil heiress who was initially a murder suspect before being rebranded as the victim of a killer con artist. Jasmine hadn't followed the story initially, but when it appeared Violet James was being hunted by a killer, her heart had gone out to the woman. Many nights, she'd awakened from a deep sleep, praying for the safety of a person she'd never met. Violet's situation was too close to Jasmine's.

She sat on the edge of the bed closest to the door. From the looks of the wrinkles in the bedspread, someone had been sleeping there. The wailing must have awakened them, too. "What was that awful noise earlier?"

Will snorted and seemed to choke on air.

Sean shot him a glare, then looked up at Jasmine. "I'm learning the harmonica. Grace likes to sing along."

For the first time in a long time, a real smile welled from her heart. Grace was a beautiful dog and, like Scout and Will, there was a genuine love between the

Akita and her owner. No, not her *owner*. She'd heard
Will say differently. Grace and Scout were *partners*.
"I'd like to see that duet."

This time, Will laughed openly. He stood and
stretched his arms overhead. "Trust me, you wouldn't."

Looking away from Will's shirt stretching over his
broad chest, Jasmine studied the place where he'd been
sitting. There was a wrapper from Friar Tuck's balled
up on the table. Her stomach let everyone in the room
know she'd seen it.

Will dropped his arms to his sides. "Hungry?"

"Yes. *Stress Eating* is my middle name. I gained
over ten pounds while I was waiting—" She stared at
her fingers and picked a cuticle. Sean still didn't know
her story. "If there's food, I'm in."

Sean stood and grabbed a sub from the refrigerator. He handed it to her as he passed. "I hope you like
ham and turkey." He looked at Will with a wry grin.
"And mayo."

"You did that on purpose?" Will threw the wrapper
at his colleague.

Sean ducked sideways then picked up two leashes
from the dresser beneath the mirror. "I'm taking Grace
outside for a walk. Want me to take Scout along?"

At the word *walk*, both dogs were on their feet.

"Well, you initiated the launch sequence, so now
you have to." Will scratched the collie's ears, then patted him firmly on the side and sent him to Sean, who
leashed both dogs and slipped out the door.

As soon as the door was shut, Will sat in the chair
the other man had vacated and pointed at the table.
"You want to eat over here?" He leaned over and pulled

a bottle of water from the small refrigerator, setting it on the table in front of the other chair.

Jasmine unwrapped the sub, blessed it, then pulled the tomatoes off and set them aside. Tomatoes were fine cooked, but raw? Ugh.

She ate three bites while Will stared at the laptop that rested near her food. Her grateful stomach felt better as soon as she swallowed the fresh bread and salty cheese and meat combination. She chased the bites with water and forced herself to slow down. "You talk to your team on the computer?"

"When we're not together." Will shoved the laptop farther to the side, giving Jasmine more space. "To answer your earlier question, yes. That meeting was about Violet James. And it will be on the news as soon as the next of kin are notified, so it won't hurt to tell you." He succinctly laid out the facts of a horrifying home invasion and murder.

Laying the sub on the table, Jasmine slowly wiped her mouth with a napkin. "I know exactly how that poor woman is feeling. She's alone and scared with no one to help her. She has a killer on her heels." Once again, the familiarity of the situation sank into her bones. Jasmine shuddered.

"You were never alone." He straightened and leaned forward, resting his hand over hers on the table. "And you're not alone now."

The warmth of his fingers, and his words, ran straight into her heart. No, she wasn't.

Jasmine let her gaze slide from Will's hand, up his arm and finally to his eyes, which washed over her intently with a look she'd seen more than once over the past day or so.

A lump rose to her throat. If she read too deeply into what he wasn't saying, she'd fall. *Hard.* "You're right." Jasmine pulled her hand from his. "I had the marshals with me before. I have you and Sean now. I'm in a much better position than Violet James is."

Will sat back and crossed his arms over his chest. His face was unreadable. For a long moment, he studied the tabletop as if contemplating what to do next. Finally, he grabbed one of the discarded tomato slices from her sub wrapper. He chewed and swallowed. "Do you think about it a lot? The murder you witnessed?"

Jasmine picked at the edge of the sub, pulling crumbs from the side. "I try not to." She shuddered and glanced at Will. "I don't know if you've ever seen anyone shot in the head."

His face revealed nothing.

She closed her eyes briefly, but it made the mental image only stronger, so she opened them and stared at the heavy curtains behind Will. "During the day, I can usually block it. But I still have nightmares about it." She chuckled, but it wasn't with amusement. More like irony and pain. "I can't even watch crime dramas on TV anymore, and I used to love them. They hit too close to home. It's bothered me more since I heard about Violet James, probably because I understand. I wonder what she saw, what she's dealing with, how she's coping. I had counselors to talk to. She has no one. At least, no one we know of."

"That's one of the reasons we want to find her. That and to protect her from the men pursuing her. It's likely she saw something. Though at this point, with so much evidence stacked against Wells and Dennis, and this double homicide that's also linked to them, what Violet

James saw in Chugach is irrelevant to whether or not they spend the rest of their lives in jail."

"Whereas I was the only one who could put Anton Rogers away. And he's still angry about it." Angry enough to kill her if he ever discovered that Jasmine Jefferson and Yasmine Carlisle were one and the same.

Will plucked another tomato from her discard pile. "I want to ask you for a favor."

Her stomach picked that moment to remind her she was still hungry. "What's that?" If it would help bring the smugglers down, she'd already committed to do whatever it took. She took another huge bite of the sub. The more she ate, the hungrier she was. Stress was going to be the end of her, no doubt.

"I'd like to take a look at your phone and see if Eli, our tech guy, can tell if you've been hacked."

"I carry a dumb phone. I never wanted to risk being traced. I can't even check email on it. Just text and call." The thought of a GPS device in her pocket gave her the heebie-jeebies.

"Computer?"

"I had a work laptop, but we're in the process of an upgrade, so Darrin asked for it back about a week ago so he could get my new one set up. My personal one is on me at all times. It's in my backpack in my room." She hated to leave it out of her sight, terrified a faceless monster might somehow figure out who she was, even though she'd been extremely careful. "I have nothing to hide from you. You can let Eli search it if you think it will help."

"One more thing." He leaned closer and clasped his hands on the table, holding her gaze, his dark eyes serious. "I'd like permission to see your WITSEC file. And, if you're okay with it, to read Sean in on your situation."

The sub stuck in her mouth. She couldn't stop chewing. If Will was asking her that, then he didn't believe Deputy Marshal Maldonado when he said her identity was safe. She stared at Will, mouth full, eyes wide, suspended in time.

He opened her water bottle and handed it to her. "Drink. I'm not fond of doing CPR."

It took several tries, but she finally managed to swallow and find her voice. "Why?" The word was thin, betraying the rising fear that made her wish she hadn't succumbed to hunger. That sub had been a huge mistake.

"I don't want you to worry or to panic. I just want to be sure we're coming at this from all angles. I can get a little bit laser sighted sometimes, only looking at one thing. A teammate reminded me of that earlier today." He scrubbed a hand down his face. "I just want to be a hundred percent certain that the shootings and the sabotage are about the drug smugglers and not about your past. My ultimate goal is to keep you safe, even if that means I don't fly with you."

"If you don't fly with me then you'll find another pilot, and I'll be—" *Alone.* She couldn't say the word. The truth was, she'd be alone eventually, whether he flew with her or not. He couldn't stay by her side forever, couldn't leave his job to play personal bodyguard to a woman who was constantly afraid. "I want you to fly with me." This wasn't about her. She'd made a verbal promise to him and one in her heart to those who were vulnerable on the frontier. She wouldn't back out.

She'd prayed too much and heard God's voice too clearly to disobey His call.

"And I want to be sure you're safe. It's no secret I don't trust Darrin or Keith. They're the ones who've likely done the most digging into your background, before they hired you. I want to know for certain that they didn't figure out who you used to be."

"There's no evidence that they have." She refused to believe it. Neither Darrin nor Keith was a killer.

"Covering all the bases. That's all. I promise." His expression was sincere.

But it did nothing to cool the fear that burned in her veins. Long ago, she'd surrendered her life to whatever God wanted of her, but some days, it felt like He wanted too much. "I think—"

The door burst open. Sean entered with both dogs, his face strained. He flicked a glance at Jasmine, then focused on Will. "We have a problem. A big one."

FOURTEEN

Will was on his feet before the words were fully out of Sean's mouth. One hand reached for his pistol while the other motioned for Jasmine to stay seated. Until he knew the full story, he needed her to stay in place. "We've been found?"

With a quick nod, Sean dropped the dogs' leashes and reached for his backpack by the door. "I had the K-9s at the side of the building, around the corner from the back parking lot and figured we'd check on the vehicles while we were out there. When we rounded the building, there was a dark blue coupe circling the lot. It stopped near your vehicle. The driver started to get out, but then he spotted me and took off."

"License plate?" Will pulled his hand away from his sidearm, but he didn't let his guard down. While the danger wasn't imminent, it could flare at any moment.

"Negative. He was headed in the wrong direction. The person's tall and built, but glare and angle kept me from getting much detail on them."

"Male or female?" Sean's hesitation to name a gender redirected Will's suspicions. They'd thought of the shooter as a male all along, but that was a dangerous game to play. He'd heard of very few female killers for hire, but they were out there.

"I'm not sure. Like I said, there was a lot working against me, but there's enough doubt for me to think we could possibly be dealing with a woman."

Jasmine cleared her throat. "Or someone who was just looking for a place to stay." Her voice was shallow, as though even she didn't believe that was the case.

It was a valiant effort at keeping her sanity in place, and Will didn't argue with her.

But he didn't believe in coincidence. Cold hard facts were what helped him and his team solve cases. It's what kept them alive. The similarity to the shooter's vehicle, the interest in their patrol SUVs and the flight at Sean's appearance all said their secret location was no longer a secret.

As the lead guy on the investigation, what happened next was his call. Sean stood by the door waiting for an order, his backpack gripped tightly in his left hand.

Like it or not, they had to move. And it was risky, but he knew the exact place they needed to go. He spoke to Jasmine first. "Pack your things. Be ready to go in five minutes."

She opened her mouth as if she was either going to argue or refuse, but then she got up and left the room, her shoulders a hard line. Rather than speak of determination or defiance, that posture spoke of false bravado, of trying to hold it together until she could safely fall apart.

Will had never wanted anything more than to follow her and to pull her into his arms. To reassure her that he wasn't going to let anything happen to her.

But he couldn't. There were no promises to make. And Sean would surely question his motives if he did.

Without having to be asked, the other man started emptying the dogs' water bowls. "I radioed it in. Fairbanks PD is going to patrol nearby, keeping an eye out for the vehicle. I don't know how far we're going to get with the description 'dark blue coupe,' but at least it's something."

"Yeah, and even if they pull the driver over, there's little cause to hold them unless they have the weapon they fired at us still in the vehicle." Will kept his voice low, hoping his words didn't reach Jasmine in the next room. He took Scout's bowl from Sean and shoved it into his backpack, along with the remains of a small bag of dog food. "The best we can do if we spot them is put a tail on them and see if they try to pull anything. Worst case scenario, they do nothing to incriminate themselves. However, if they think we're onto them, they may lie low for a bit and take some of the heat off Jasmine."

Sean tossed his backpack on the bed and grabbed his duffel, shoving his shaving kit into it. "Or this is a ploy. A distraction. An attempt to flush us out."

That was the thing nagging at the back of Will's mind. There could be more than one person on the hunt for Jasmine and for the troopers leading the charge on the smuggling investigation. Or there could be a lone wolf who was operating for Anton Rogers and looking for a quick payday.

There was no consistency to the would-be killer's tactics. They were savvy enough to rig a plane's engine on the fly, but foolish and reckless enough to take potshots in broad daylight from the same position twice.

They were either overly confident and brazen, or they were a careless newbie out to make a buck and to buy themselves some street cred.

Will wasn't sure which one was more dangerous. "Whoever this is was able to sabotage Jasmine's plane, either at the airfield or while she was unloading at one of her stops. We have to assume we're dealing with a professional."

"Which means they could have rigged one of our vehicles while we were inside." Sean was already headed for the door. "Maya's six hours away, so we can't get her here with Sarge in time to sniff for explosives. A tracking device might be hard to spot. I'll see if I can spot anything out of the ordinary. We'll have to pray for the best beyond that." He reached down, grabbed Grace's leash and was gone before Will could stop him.

As soon as the door closed behind Sean, Jasmine stepped in carrying her backpack and a gym bag. "Where are we going?"

"I'll tell you when we get in the car and we're on the way." He couldn't risk the room having been bugged in their absence. The only safe house he could think of at the moment belonged to a former army buddy who'd been stationed at Fort Wainwright. He was deployed at the moment, but Will had crashed at his place before and knew where there was a spare key. While he hadn't wanted to risk using a buddy's home as a safe house before, they were running out of options now.

The trick would be getting to the house undetected, which would be tough given how conspicuous their SUVs were. But, if he remembered correctly, Kelvin had a garage. That would help. And he'd have a washer and dryer, and a yard for the dogs.

Although, hopefully, they would bring down their killer and their smuggler and they wouldn't have to stay for very long.

He started to tell Jasmine they'd leave as soon as Sean returned, but as he opened his mouth, he really saw her for the first time since she'd stepped into the room. Her face was pale. Her mouth was tight.

This time, he couldn't stop himself from going to her and offering comfort. Everything about her situation tugged at his heart. Dropping his backpack onto the bed, he closed the space between them and pulled her to him. "It's going to be okay."

"Is it? Because it doesn't feel that way." Her mouth moved against his shoulder, her words so low he wouldn't have caught them if they'd been spoken any farther from his ear.

He wanted to tell her he was doing the best he could. That he'd put himself between a bullet and her if he had to. Of course, he'd do that for any civilian, wouldn't he?

Adrenaline shot through his heart and quaked into his veins. He'd protect anyone who needed him, but he'd rather die than know he'd failed Jasmine. If he failed her, he wouldn't be able to take it, not just because he'd allowed something to happen to her on his watch…

But because he couldn't imagine a world without her.

Involuntarily, his arms tightened around her, and he laid his cheek against her hair. Somehow, without his permission, she'd found her way into his heart.

The emotion ached from the inside out. He couldn't do this. He couldn't *feel* this. It went against everything he knew to be true. She'd use him. Hurt him. Turn her back on him.

Yet despite everything, he couldn't believe any of

that was true about Jasmine. It made no sense he'd feel this way. He'd known her for only a few days.

But he'd handed her pieces of himself and of his story that he'd never offered to another living soul.

And she'd protected them, even seemed to cherish them.

She *saw* him. Really saw him. And she treated him in ways Beth never had. In ways no one else ever had.

And now, he—

Running footsteps outside shattered his emotional rambling. Dropping his arms, he backed away from Jasmine and stood between her and the door, hand near his weapon, ready to draw if danger came knocking.

But it was Sean and Grace who entered, and his face was even grimmer than before.

He tossed his keys to Will, who caught them overhanded. "Take my car. Go." He glanced at Jasmine and winced. "There's an explosive device under the passenger seat of your vehicle on the exterior. I've called EOD here in Fairbanks. Get her to safety. *Now.*"

This was the thing Jasmine feared the most.

She sat on the sofa with her head in her hands, staring down at the beige carpet in a duplex that belonged to Will's army friend. The blinds were closed. The door was locked. In the neighborhood around the duplex, plainclothes state troopers stood watch. She didn't know how many.

Will had taken her laptop when they arrived here and had wired it into a secure router he produced from that infinitely deep backpack of his.

If things weren't so serious, she'd call him Mary Poppins.

From some remote location far away, his teammate Eli was scanning her hard drive, searching for clues to what she might know. If her brain couldn't reveal it, maybe her computer's storage could.

Or maybe she didn't know anything. Maybe Anton Rogers had managed to find her and exact his revenge.

It was so much like when she'd been asked to testify. Everything was upside down and out of control. Her life was no longer hers...again. Someone was definitely trying to kill her...again. She would likely have to change her name...again.

It had been a vague fear before, but now the horror had come to fruition. Bullets flying toward her at the airfield were one thing. They could be attributed to local drug smugglers simply trying to take her out for knowing something she honestly didn't know she knew.

But a bomb? Under a state trooper's SUV? That was the exact reason she'd been offered protection in the first place, a bomb wired to her beloved Ford Bronco.

It felt like Rogers was sending her a message, one that said she'd better enjoy every breath, because each one might be her last.

Now her worst nightmares were really coming true. She wouldn't even be able to fly as scheduled tomorrow, not with her life and the lives of everyone around her in danger.

Worse, once the federal marshals took over her protection, Will would likely be off duty.

The one person she trusted, the one person she counted as a real friend who truly knew her, would be gone, never to be seen again.

Jasmine wrapped her arms around her stomach. That pain might be the worst of all. She'd allowed herself to

her job, but who she was inside. No matter what happened with WITSEC, she would always be herself inside. And she'd have Jesus. She would always be who *He* said she was, no matter what the world thought.

And she'd also always have the memory of this man, who could have been so much more to her if life had been different.

When she'd left her family behind and been told to avoid contact, her heart had been torn in two. She was left without her loved ones, without her support system. Jasmine would never know her brother's children or get to be with her parents as they aged. That was a grief she still carried every day.

But the idea of leaving Will behind and never being able to contact him again was a different kind of pain. It was a ripping tear that threatened to steal her breath. How could it be that a man she'd met only a few days ago had lodged himself so deeply inside of her that it felt like her heart would be left in tatters when he was gone?

"Jas?" Will's voice was low, barely a whisper and ragged with an emotion her soul recognized and gravitated toward.

She realized she'd been staring at him as her thoughts ran wild. That somehow, she'd locked eyes with him without even realizing it. He was bound to be able to see every whirling, spinning thought she was thinking.

And she didn't care.

Narrowing his eyes as though he was trying to make sense of what he saw, Will tightened his fingers around hers. He brushed her hair from her face, tucking it behind her ear. His thumb lingered against her cheek, then dropped to trace her lower lip. His eyes followed, then lifted to look into hers, asking for permission.

Jasmine gave a slight nod and met him halfway.

It had been years since she'd kissed a man. Since she'd dated. Or simply allowed herself to let go. And in this moment, all the joy and wonder that she hadn't been able to feel for so long unlocked and exploded in her chest, flowing between her and Will. Her free hand grabbed the front of his shirt and held on, not wanting him to leave. Not wanting to lose him.

Not wanting to retreat into the emptiness that had engulfed her for too long.

FIFTEEN

Will silenced every alarm bell that tried to ring in his head. He no longer wanted to think. Thinking had landed him in a vast frontier all alone, cynical and cold-hearted for too long. Right now, all he wanted to do was to feel the things that his past had denied him for too much of his life.

He wrapped his hand around Jasmine's on his chest and held on, pouring his heart into hers. There wasn't a time he could ever remember truly feeling, not since he was a little kid. Kissing this woman was like the warmth of a childhood summer afternoon. Calm, warm, yet exhilarating with all the possibilities life had to offer.

He hadn't realized how isolated and closed off he'd been until this moment. He never wanted to leave.

But the alarm bells rang louder.

Jasmine gasped and pulled away suddenly, as though she could hear them, too. "Will."

The sound wasn't coming from his mind. That noise was *real*, and it came from his phone.

Will tore his gaze from hers. He'd forgotten who he was, who *she* was, where they were and what they were doing.

He'd forgotten that her life rested in his hands.

"Jasmine, I—" There was really nothing he could say. He'd overstepped. Allowed his heart to rule the show for the first time in recent memory. It had been incredible.

But he couldn't let it happen again.

Disengaging his hand from hers, he pulled his phone from the holster at his hip and pivoted away from her as he answered. "Stryker."

"I've found something." Eli sounded like he was out of breath.

It must be good. Nothing got the tech guru more excited than finding something technical that someone else wanted to keep hidden. Will was on his feet. "A *something* that's going to break open my case?"

"Maybe. If I'm right, it might be enough to get you a broader search warrant and enough evidence to put this thing to rest. You may want to get Jasmine and get to her computer. She'll be able to explain a couple of things to me that I need to put some pieces into place. I'll see if my theory holds any water then."

Will looked over his shoulder at Jasmine, who sat on the couch, watching him. Her expression was guarded. He swallowed the need to discuss what had just happened. It would have to wait, even though it felt like the most immediate issue in his world at the moment.

He tipped the phone down, away from his mouth. "Eli's found something. Wants you to grab your laptop and walk him through a few things."

Pressing her hands against her knees, she rose slowly then followed him into the kitchen, where the laptop sat on the island, hooked to a secure hotspot Will had set up.

He laid his phone on the counter next to the laptop and hit the button to put the device on speaker. "We're both here and we can both hear you."

"Let's rock and roll." Eli had remoted into the laptop from his office in Anchorage after Will downloaded an app the other man had perfected. Eli was able to control the machine as if he sat in front of it.

It always freaked him out a little to watch the cursor seemingly move by itself. Windows opened and shifted on the screen to form a square. He pressed his palms against his thighs to keep his hands from reaching for the laptop.

Beside him, Jasmine shuddered, probably feeling that same sense of eeriness. She watched the screen for a moment then leaned forward, her brow furrowed. Her hand moved toward the laptop's track pad, then hesitated and dropped back to her side. "Wait. Eli?"

"Yes?" His voice held an uptick that said he already knew what she'd seen.

"That box on the top right. Can you make it bigger? Full screen?"

As if her words had sway with the computer, the requested window filled the screen.

Lips pursed, she studied what appeared to be a schedule built on a spreadsheet.

"Tell me what you see." Eli was searching for something, it was clear. Like any good investigator, he wanted to hear it from the witness, not direct their thoughts in any particular direction.

"That's the flight schedule. Darrin usually sends us a file for each week and emails it out to us on Fridays. This is his full spreadsheet, though, for the rest of the year. He hasn't sent that before. I'd have noticed this flight schedule sooner, but I haven't bothered to look at it, since I'm off next week." Her elbow bumped Will's arm as she pointed at the screen. "I've never seen it color coded like this, though. Eli, can you scroll to this week?"

The view shifted, and Will studied the spreadsheet that appeared. Days and times ran across the top, corresponding with the current week. Locations ran down the left side. Several names filled the grids, but Jasmine's and Keith's stood out to him. Of Keith's four flights, three were highlighted in green: the one he'd departed with this morning, one scheduled for takeoff the next morning and the one that coincided with the flight Jasmine had taken earlier in the week, when Will had boarded her plane.

His eyes narrowed. Jasmine's flight, the one he'd received the anonymous tip on, was highlighted in orange.

"What's that?" Jasmine aimed a finger at Keith's flight from today.

"What's *what*?" There was no way for Eli to see what she was doing, a fact that was easy to forget in a situation like this.

"Zoom in on Keith's flight for today. Make it bigger." She flapped her hand in front of her as though she was impatient to do the work herself. "It looks like there's something in small print in that cell under his name."

The indicated cell zoomed in until it took up most of the real estate on the screen. Keith's name loomed large on the highlighted green cell. Underneath, in the tiniest of fonts, was a note. *AAS 543 Kod.*

Will pulled his phone from his pocket and scanned the text the colonel had sent him earlier, detailing the anonymous tip that had come in. "Eli, look up Ammituq Air Service out of Kodiak. See if 543 means anything."

The only sound over the line was the tapping of Eli's keyboard, then he drew a deep breath. "According to their published schedule, 543 is a small freight and passenger flight that flew out this morning at 8:27, headed for Cold Bay."

Will fought the urge to pump his fist in the air. The Ammituq flight's time coincided with Keith's green-highlighted flight from this morning, if he hadn't taken off early. He scrolled to his case notes and looked at the screen again. "Roll back another week, Eli."

"On it."

Will waited as the spreadsheet updated, and another green highlight appeared. Keith's highlighted flight had lifted off at the exact time as the Sea-Bush Air flight he had investigated the week before. "Make Keith's green flight bigger." Once again, the flight number matched the anonymous tip.

Jasmine gasped, her hand going to her mouth. Clearly, she'd seen the same condemning evidence that Will and Eli had seen. Every anonymous tip lined up with a highlighted flight piloted by Keith Hawkins. Green for money, for smuggling runs. Jasmine's was the only flight in orange, because it was their own, one they'd tagged to deflect suspicion from themselves.

Will dragged a hand down his face, scrubbing against a day's worth of stubble. Darrin was the one trying to kill Jasmine. There was no other explanation. Once he realized he'd emailed her his master list, he'd decided had no other choice.

Will had found his smugglers...and his smoking gun.

* * *

Hand to her mouth, Jasmine stepped away from the counter and sank onto the bar stool behind her. Her throat tightened. There was no way she was seeing what she was on that screen. Her heart refused to believe it.

But her mind couldn't deny it.

Darrin maintained the flight schedule. Keith piloted those flights.

Beside her, Will continued to speak to Eli, but their words buzzed around her head in an incoherent babble. Her senses couldn't take everything in all at once. They could only see. See that Keith's mysteriously highlighted flights lined up perfectly with the anonymous tips that had led to her plane being boarded this week and Kramer Anderson's being boarded the week before. To other flights that had been targeted in the past.

Darrin and Keith had used her. Had pointed the Alaska State Troopers in her direction. *On purpose*. To throw the scent off their trail.

To make unreal amounts of money by destroying the lives of people on the Alaskan frontier.

How many flights had Keith made? How much had he ferried on each flight? How many people had he pointed the finger of false accusation at?

And he was still flying.

Wait. "What about the flight this morning?"

Will broke off from whatever he was saying to Eli to address her. "We had a tip come in last night, but it was lost in the shuffle of the happenings in the Violet James case."

At this very moment, Keith was likely distributing tens of thousands of dollars' worth of illegal drugs. Jasmine grabbed Will's arm. "We have to go get him."

His sigh was heavy. "I'll call you back in a minute, Eli." He punched the end call button, then slipped free of Jasmine's grasp and wrapped both of his arms around her, pulling her close until she rested her head against his shoulder.

She couldn't relax against him. Her mind was too blown.

Will swallowed so hard she could hear it. There was no doubt he'd do anything to take this pain away from her. He'd been working with Sean to protect her from physical harm, but no one had stopped to think what might happen to her emotionally. What it might do to her to know that her bosses were not who they seemed.

How it would feel to be facing down murderous drug runners. *Again.*

Will shook his head. "It's too late to go after Keith today. According to the schedule, he's due back in an hour. He'll have already dropped off whatever he was hauling. But we know where he flew, and Eli is getting in touch with the colonel to get some of our people into those areas ASAP to see what we can uncover and how much we can round up."

"But we can't afford to wait!" She pulled away from him and looked up into his eyes. "Will, he flies again *tomorrow.*"

"And he has no idea we've seen this yet." Will guided her onto the bar stool, then perched on the one beside hers, holding her right hand loosely in his. "I have a theory."

She stared down at her hand in his but didn't say anything. As much as she could still feel his lips on hers, and as much as she'd like to lean in and find comfort in his arms again, now was not the right time.

"I think Darrin accidentally sent you the wrong file. That's why he took your work laptop. That's why your apartment was trashed. He was looking for your personal laptop. He knew you couldn't access your email from your phone, so his only hope was to delete his mistake from your laptop before you could see it."

"I don't know." Jasmine shook her head. How could this be happening?

"Jas, Eli found that file in an email that had been deleted from your inbox, but not from the main server. I think Darrin couldn't take the chance that you'd seen it or that deleting it from your work laptop would guarantee it was gone from your personal one."

"So he tried to kill me before I could log on." Her words were barely a breath. The more she considered her situation, the more her lungs refused to expand.

He hesitated, and his fingers tightened around hers. "It's possible. The attempts on your life didn't start until the day after the email was sent. He had time to sabotage the plane before you took off, though I'm not sure how mechanically inclined he is."

"He used to service all the planes before we hired Jerry. He could easily have made a mess of my plane." She swallowed against emotion that tried to choke her. "But he didn't have time to get to the edge of the airfield to shoot at me."

"True. But there could be some other factors at play, other players in the game. They could have partners, or they could have hired someone. Eli will do that Dark Web thing he does and see if he can find any evidence that the Hawkins brothers put a call out for a—" He clamped down on the words Jasmine had hoped she'd never hear again. *Hired assassin.*

His thumb drew a small circle on her wrist, somehow comforting and disconcerting all at the same time. There was nothing she could do. Darrin had no idea whether or not she'd seen that email, and he would keep coming at her.

But Jasmine couldn't focus on herself right now. There were so many bigger factors to think about. "The way he's acting, he doesn't believe we've seen it yet. That means he has no idea that you know about tomorrow's flight. He might be greedy enough to take the risk of making the delivery."

"Which gives us time to set up an operation to catch them in the act, assuming they don't get too cautious and scrap the shipment. I'm guessing that, if there's enough money at stake, they'll still make the flight." Reaching for her other hand, Will held both between them. "If all goes well, by this time tomorrow, you'll be safe."

"With no job. No security." She lifted her eyes to his. Either she kept her mouth shut to avoid possible humiliation, or she took a risk and spoke what was in her heart. After the way he'd just kissed her, if she was going to make a leap, it was now or never. "And no you."

Will seemed to stop breathing. His gaze dipped down and to the left, to something under the lip of the bar where they sat.

To anywhere other than her eyes.

Somehow, she'd read the situation wrong. She'd been that foolish woman who fell for the hero who was only doing his job.

Except he'd kissed her.

Maybe it had just been a moment for him. Maybe they were both overly emotional. Maybe if she got a good night's sleep, she'd wake up with Will Stryker out of her system.

Jasmine pulled her hands from his. If she couldn't take the words back, she could try to make them less humiliating. "I just meant that you're the only one who knows about me. I'd hate to lose you as a friend. That's all I'm saying."

She stood and turned her back on Will. "I'm going to try to get some sleep." Not that she'd be able to relax, but she couldn't bear to be in his presence any longer.

"Jasmine, wait." Behind her, it was easy to tell he had stood.

But Jasmine didn't stop. She kept walking, up the stairs, and away from Will Stryker.

SIXTEEN

The sun had just begun to peek over the edges of the horizon, filtering dim light over the quiet airfield. With one knee on the ground and the other bent for stability, Will surveyed the area. Around him, Sean and other members of the K-9 team who had been able to assemble on short notice concealed themselves in various hiding places, along with several DEA agents who had been called in and were taking point on the raid. It seemed no one was willing to blow this bust.

After yesterday's discoveries, he'd obtained a warrant and had Eli find a way into the Kesuk Aviation computers as well as into any personal devices that could be linked to the brothers. Sean had been instrumental in helping Eli last night, entering the building under the cover of darkness to work from this end. Hopefully, their tech equipment would yield even more answers than today's operation.

Beside Will, Scout sat quietly. His rigid muscles and nose in the air said he sensed the tension and adrenaline as he waited for a command. Hopefully, it wouldn't be much longer. They would come in behind the initial raid to sweep the plane for the drugs Will was certain Keith and Darrin were hiding.

Will adjusted Scout's small bulletproof vest. His partner wasn't fond of it, especially on warm days. At least in the dawn hours, the temperature hovered around fifty, so there was no chance of the dog overheating. There was no way Will would let him into the fray without gear. He'd do all he could to protect his partner and friend.

Just like he'd do all he could to protect Jasmine, who was also his...

Friend was no longer the right word. His finger tapped the grip of his Glock. He had never been one to kiss and run. His faith was ingrained too deeply for frivolous relationships.

He sensed she lived the same way, with the added weight of her identity to bear. A kiss for either of them was more than the cheap thing the world had made of it.

He had no idea what to do with that. That moment between them was so much more than two people who were happy to find friends. It was...

Impossible. There was no way he'd fallen for her so quickly. His history said that was a foolish idea.

Yet leaving her this morning in the care of his team member Poppy Walsh and her Irish wolfhound, Stormy, had been one of the hardest things he'd ever done. Jasmine had merely stood at the top of the stairs and looked down as he'd prepared to leave. She hadn't spoken since she'd walked away the day before, all because he'd lost his words when she'd laid her heart at his feet. Her confession had shocked him more than their kiss. He'd wanted to pull her close and promise her forever.

He couldn't. Not when her life was up in the air and his was filled with duty and danger.

His radio earpiece crackled and drew him to his mission. Sean's voice was low in the transmission. "Targets on-site. One vehicle. Navy blue Expedition. Both entering building."

Will drew deeper into the shadows, as he was sure the entire assembled team did. They'd better be right about this. Keith and Darrin needed to load that plane in the next fifteen minutes or the entire operation would collapse when they lost the cover of predawn darkness.

Trooper Helena Maddox's voice came across the radio. "Target one approaching hangar. Target two crossing north side of airfield to storage shed." Where she waited with her partner, Luna, a Norwegian elkhound trained in suspect apprehension, she had a view straight down the runway.

From across the runway, the scrape of an opening hangar door tore through the morning stillness. Darrin appeared, opening a small storage shed on the far side of the hangar.

Will and Scout had made a cursory exterior search of the small shed earlier. It was different than the others on the property, a sturdier construction, likely to keep sniffers like his partner from detecting what was inside.

Will flexed his fingers, then scratched Scout behind the ear. *Just a few more minutes, buddy.* Hopefully, today's search would turn up all the evidence they needed.

"Wait for them to load the plane. Move on my signal." A DEA agent Will hadn't met before spoke the orders. "Perimeter doesn't detect any other movement on-site."

The brothers were acting alone. No backup waited to blast in and take out the team when they moved in. Will breathed a sigh of relief as the moments ticked past and the brothers carted crates to the plane. He'd been on raids before, but this one had his palms sweating and his muscles itching to move. This one was *personal*. These men had tried to harm the woman he loved.

The realization nearly rocked him to the side, but there was no time to unpack the emotion because his radio hissed. "On my mark."

Will focused on the scene, where the two men loaded the last crate onto the King Air. As soon as Keith slid the door shut, Will's earpiece exploded with sound. "Move! Move! Move!"

Will eased forward, weapon ready. He would provide perimeter support while the main team went in. Like a well-oiled machine, troopers and agents crept from the shadows toward the two men who, until now, had been oblivious to their presence.

"Drug Enforcement agents executing a warrant! Lock your fingers behind your heads and get on your knees!" The scene erupted as nearly a dozen law enforcement officers converged on the brothers.

Darrin and Keith froze. For a second, it seemed Darrin was going to run, but then he took in the overwhelming number of men and women surrounding them and slowly lifted his hands.

Keith hesitated, but as the team drew closer and their sheer number and firepower became obvious, he complied as well.

Along with several other members of his team, Will hovered around the edges to provide cover as the DEA took the men into custody.

Once they were secured, he holstered his pistol and approached with Scout. He let his partner off the leash, hefted him into the King Air, and commanded the K-9 to search. His partner stopped at the first crate he sniffed and began to paw at the hasp lock, an active alert that there were narcotics present.

Busted.

He shot a hard look at Darrin, who stood off to the side in handcuffs and surrounded by federal agents. "Is there paperwork for the drugs in these containers? Is this a legal shipment?"

Darrin responded with a defiant glare.

There was so much Will wanted to say, so many things he wanted to unleash on the man who'd lied to Jasmine, who'd used her and had put her life in danger.

Who'd tried to murder her, simply because he'd mistakenly sent her the wrong attachment in an email.

Fists clenched, Will bit back the words and faced Keith instead. Given the man's propensity for disappearing when law enforcement was around, he was likely the weak link. "Key?"

Before his eyes, Keith seemed to deflate. His shoulders slouched forward, the mark of a man who knew he had nowhere to hide. "My right jacket pocket."

Behind him, Darrin spewed a series of violent curse words, likely meant to burn his brother alive.

The trooper closest to Keith fished out the key and passed it to the nearest DEA agent, who climbed into the plane and opened the box. "I'm looking at fentanyl, and what appears to be heroin."

Definitely busted.

The agents near the plane didn't need Scout, so Will crossed the tarmac toward the lead agent. "Ma'am, I'd like to get my partner into that building." He tipped his chin at the shed that Darrin and Keith had been in earlier. "I know you don't need us to go in, but I'd love to finish what I started." He wanted to see this through to the very end.

Agent Reeves nodded, and her red ponytail swung from the movement. "I can understand that, Trooper." She motioned to a small contingent of agents, and they trekked to the thick-walled metal building. A few moments later, she produced a ring of keys. "We got these off the foul-mouthed brother. He wasn't happy to part with them."

The third key opened the door, and Will unleashed Scout. His partner entered the empty building and almost immediately sat in the middle of the floor. Will smiled grimly and tossed his expectant partner a treat. The crates were already on the plane and being searched, but there was satisfaction in knowing he'd found his men.

"Did you get the closure you needed?" Agent Reeves stepped up beside Will and watched Scout, who still sat in the darkened shed. "Now we just have to track who's bringing the cargo into this airfield. I'm guessing Keith Hawkins will lay out some information for a deal. He doesn't seem like the type to hold back if he thinks he can finagle a lighter prison sentence."

Will glanced over at the brothers, one who was staring at his shoes and the other who glared with malice at whoever caught his eye. "And Darrin is the type to take the hard way out. He'll hit prison and think he can take over."

"He'll learn a hard lesson." Agent Reeves twisted her lip as she studied the brothers. Then she gave Will a curt nod. "You and your partner have done some good work here, Trooper. This is going to land some bigger fish than you thought when you started tracking these guys."

As Agent Reeves returned to her team, Will called Scout over and knelt to reward him with another treat and more pets than the dog could handle.

Scout rolled over onto his back for a coveted belly rub.

With his first genuine smile of the day, Will complied. "Yeah, you earned it, buddy." When his phone buzzed at his hip, he continued scratching Scout's neck with one hand while he pulled the phone to his ear with the other. "Stryker."

"Will, it's Eli."

The tension in Eli's voice stilled Will's hand. He rocked back on his heels. "What's going on?"

"The colonel got a call from WITSEC concerning Jasmine. Did you know she was a protected witness?"

"Yes." Will's eyes squeezed closed. "She told me."

"Well, there's a team of marshals headed to Jasmine's location, but you're closer."

No. This was going to be bad. Very bad. And just when he'd thought the danger was behind them. "What's happened?"

Eli cleared his throat. "Are you near the Hawkins brothers?"

He stood as the DEA team herded the two men to a waiting SUV. "About fifty yards away."

"They're in custody?"

"Yes. Why?"

"So you don't do something you'll regret." Eli's voice was grim.

Will snapped Scout's leash to the harness and rose, watching the SUV ease down the runway away from him. "Spit it out, Eli." He was already walking, headed for his vehicle. He caught Sean's eye and gestured for his teammate to follow.

"A marshal named Maldonado asked us to look into some emails. He thought our cases might be connected. I should have figured out then that he'd already talked to you. How else would he know?"

"Know what, Eli?"

Eli's exhale was loud enough to hear over the phone. "Darrin is clearly all about the money. Keith followed along. It's all in his email trail and internet histories. He's greedy enough to be dangerous, and I found evidence he's been trolling the Dark Web for moneymaking opportunities."

Will's feet froze to the tarmac next to the main hangar. He already knew where this was going. "Anton Rogers put out a hit on Jasmine and Darrin found it."

"Worse."

Will broke into a run, already headed for his vehicle. Whatever Eli was about to reveal, it meant danger for Jasmine. "What?" He motioned for Sean to follow as he sprinted past his teammate.

"Rogers was beaten to death this morning. It was a coordinated hit." Eli's voice was heavy. "Dasha Melnyk, the cartel leader Anton and Jasmine are responsible for taking down, is alive. She's the one Darrin reached out to on the Dark Web. And, Will? Intel says she's in Alaska."

Jasmine paced from the kitchen table, past the bar and into the open living room, running her hand along the back of the sofa as she passed. When she reached the stairs, she pivoted on her heel and headed back the way she came. She had a vise grip on a coffee mug that had been drained dry half an hour earlier. Her body really didn't need any more caffeine, but she had no idea what to do with her hands if she set the mug aside, so she kept it close.

From her seat at the dining room table near the kitchen door, Trooper Poppy Walsh watched with an amused spark to her expression, then turned back to the laptop she'd been glued to since this morning's operation began.

Jasmine proceeded into the kitchen and paused in front of the window. The blinds were closed. This was exactly like the caged animal feeling of her initial flight into WITSEC. Or maybe she was restless because Will was in harm's way and she had no idea of his status. She wanted to ask Poppy, but as a civilian, that probably wasn't information she was allowed to know.

Lord, keep him safe. Keep Sean safe. Keep all of the men and women at the airfield safe. The same plea cycled through her head with every step.

She poked the blinds and headed into the living area again.

Poppy looked up and raised one eyebrow. "Will's buddy might expense us for the groove you're wearing in his hardwood floor." A gentle smile erased any censure. She bent down and scratched her Irish wolfhound partner behind the ears.

The massive dog rolled onto her back, ready for a tummy rub, but Poppy petted her on the side and straightened, cocking her head as she listened to the radio in her ear.

Jasmine froze as the trooper's expression shifted. Her

grip on the coffee mug grew tighter. The thick ceramic just might give way soon.

With a nod, Poppy found Jasmine's gaze. "They have Darrin and Keith in custody. Everybody's safe."

Exhaling a breath she hadn't realized she was holding, Jasmine sank into a chair across the table from Poppy and settled the empty mug in front of her. *Thank You, Lord*. It was over. The supply line had been cut. She was safe from anonymous shooters and bomb makers.

It was over. The relief evaporated in a new kind of tension. Her job was gone. Her friends had betrayed her. Will would leave with his team as early as this afternoon.

"Will filled me in on some of your situation."

Jasmine's head snapped up. Surely he hadn't told his team that she was living under the government's protection. "How much?"

"You're close to Darrin and Keith, and they put you in danger. Will hinted that there was more he couldn't tell." Poppy chewed her lower lip, then slid the laptop across the table. She adjusted her earpiece, seeming to stall before she spoke. "He also hinted some things about himself."

"Is he okay?" Suddenly, her life wasn't so important. Will's was. If anything had happened to him…

"He's fine." Poppy smiled, but then she winced. "He wouldn't talk to me for a week if he knew I was saying this."

Jasmine leaned forward. Whatever Poppy was about to reveal, she had a feeling it was going to change everything.

"I've known Will for a while. He's a cynical guy who

doesn't trust easily. He was wounded pretty badly in his past. I know part of the story, but I don't know all of it."

"He told me."

Poppy's eyebrow arched over green eyes. It seemed she was going to speak, but then she scanned the laptop screen. When she looked up, her expression had reset to neutral. "Will's not a big talker."

Could have fooled her. He'd talked *a lot* and had managed to get her to open up as well.

"I'll just say this. Will trusts you." Poppy tapped her index finger on the table, as though she was trying to put words to her thoughts. "We've partnered on cases. Trained our dogs together. The whole team has. It took months for him to trust us." When she looked straight into Jasmine's eyes, there was a hint of warning. "I don't know what tomorrow is going to bring, but don't take Will's trust for granted."

"I won't." Poppy had handed her a gift. Jasmine wouldn't take that for granted either.

"I know. You don't seem like the type." The other woman smiled and started to say something else, but then she tilted her head as though she was listening. Her gaze shifted from Jasmine to the laptop, then to the ceiling, as though she could read the words being spoken into her earpiece. Furrows deepened around her mouth and along her forehead. She tipped her head and spoke into the mic at her shoulder. "Do you have an ETA?"

Jasmine watched her carefully. Something was wrong.

When Poppy closed her laptop, Jasmine blurted out, "Tell me Will's okay. Did something—" A crash came from the rear of the house, on the far side of the kitchen.

Heart leaping into double time, she jerked toward the sound.

Poppy and Stormy were on their feet before the echo faded. "It's probably a critter in the garbage cans. Take cover in the stairwell and wait for me to come back." Although the trooper's words were light, one hand went to the gun on her hip while the other went to the radio mic on her shoulder.

There was no way Poppy believed the sound was an animal.

Time slowed. Jasmine's limbs felt as though her clothes were soaked in concrete. Moving across the room was the stuff of frequent nightmares, of being chased but not being able to move fast enough to get away. Somehow, she made it to the stairwell and dropped onto the fourth step, hugging her knees to her chest.

Maybe she was overreacting. Poppy had said it was an animal, and why would she lie? Any second, she would be back and they could continue their unexpected girl chat. *Please, God.*

Outside, Poppy shouted something, but the words weren't discernible. There was a chaotic rumble of noise, almost as though a fight had broken out. Stormy barked then yelped.

Then silence.

Jasmine jumped up as footsteps sounded in the kitchen.

Lord, let those footsteps be Poppy's.

But they weren't. She would have strode in with authority. These steps were slow and deliberate. Methodical.

A predator stalking its prey.

She'd been found. The rocket shot of adrenaline from her heart to her fingertips left no doubt. Without stopping to consider her actions, Jasmine ran up the stairs, desperate for shelter, her mind screaming prayers for safety. For Poppy and for Stormy. She couldn't bear the idea of the heroic trooper and her partner lying dead because of her.

Jasmine slipped into the master bedroom, furious with herself for panicking. She should have made a run for the front door and the residential street. Instead, she'd effectively trapped herself on the second floor.

She surveyed the bedroom, desperate for a place to hide. Every space was a dead giveaway. In a closet, under the bed, in the bathtub… The killer downstairs would search those places first.

"Jasmine?" From downstairs, a woman called up.

Poppy? Jasmine turned toward the door but stopped. No. That wasn't the trooper. This voice had a faintly European accent and held a taunting lilt.

"Jasmine? We can make this easy, or we can make this hard." The voice grew louder, as though the woman stood at the bottom of the stairs. "Or should I call you Yasmine?"

Yasmine.

She hadn't heard that name spoken for two years.

Jasmine's breath caught, and she nearly whimpered. She'd been found. Anton Rogers knew where she was and had sent a killer.

No matter how this day ended, she was a dead woman.

But she wasn't going to run this time. She was not going to die easily. She whirled and searched for anything that could be used as a weapon. There was nothing. No vase like in the movies. No letter opener. Just scattered change on top of the dresser.

"Let's not drag this out," the voice called again. "Anton failed to finish you, so I'll have to do it myself."

Jasmine's knees threatened to drop her to the carpet. This was no hired killer. It was so much worse. Dasha Melnyk was alive, and she was determined to carry out revenge. No assassin for hire would be as determined as the woman Jasmine had helped to ruin.

Will needed to get here. Poppy needed to rush in. Sean needed to save the day. There had to be someone coming to get her.

But Will and Sean were at the airfield. And Poppy had gone outside and hadn't returned.

Jasmine was alone.

Maybe there was something in the closet.

"Jasmine?" The voice came closer, calm and almost playful, as though they were playing hide and seek. From the sound of it, the woman was halfway up the stairs now. "Come out, come out wherever you are. I've waited a long time to find you."

Carefully, she crept toward the closet. There had to be something in there that would—

A grim, triumphant smile edged the corner of her mouth up. A polished cypress stump with a ranger tab carved into the wood rested proudly on the floor at the end of the dresser. A little over two feet long, it was wide at the base and narrow at the top. It was a familiar souvenir. Her brother owned one just like it, the proud symbol that he'd survived swamp phase of ranger school and hadn't been taken down by the broken off cypress trees that hid in the water.

From experience, she knew the polished wood was

about the weight of a baseball bat. It would make the perfect weapon.

Jasmine hefted the stump and made her way to the door, taking up a position that would give her a slight edge of surprise.

She wasn't going to lose her life without a fight.

Not this time.

SEVENTEEN

"Poppy?" Will tried to keep his voice level as he called into the radio for his teammate, but there was no answer. His hands gripped the steering wheel tighter, and he glanced in the rearview, where Sean and Grace were trailing close behind. "Walsh? Answer me."

Silence. There hadn't been another word from Poppy in the two minutes since she'd radioed that she was headed to the back door to check on a noise outside.

Will's foot pressed the accelerator closer to the floor, and he navigated the turns in the neighborhood as quickly as he dared, Sean keeping pace behind him.

Dasha Melnyk was at the house. He had no doubt. They'd called for backup from Fairbanks PD and nearby troopers, but the combination of the airfield bust and a massive accident at the Johansen Expressway and University Avenue had tied up local resources.

His muscles were tense, and hot fear blew across his skin. He was thirty seconds from the house and he had no plan. No intel. *Nothing.*

Only the deepest gut feeling that Jasmine's time was ticking down faster than he could drive. If Melnyk had reached Anton in prison, there was no doubt she would kill Jasmine as well.

He slowed when the duplex came into sight, resisting the urge to blast up in front of the house in a screech of smoke and tires. That would only alert Melnyk.

Or it would send Poppy out with her weapon at the ready if this was just a radio glitch and she was on high alert.

As much as he wanted to rush in, he let the SUV roll to a stop a couple of houses away from duplex. He slipped from the vehicle with a reassuring word to Scout, who he left secured in his climate-controlled kennel. There was no need to drag his partner into a situation he wasn't trained for.

Silently, Sean parked his SUV behind Will's and exited the vehicle, meeting Will at the small space between the two SUVs. He, too, left his partner secured.

"Poppy's not communicating?" Sean's voice was low. He surveyed the front of the duplex, and his eyes scanned the side yard as well.

Will followed his gaze. Nothing moved. There was no indication as to what was happening behind those drawn blinds and closed curtains. "Nothing since she went to investigate a noise out back."

"So we're going in without intel."

Will's thoughts matched his teammate's somber tone. They had no way of knowing what was happening on the other side of those doors. "Poppy's last known location was the exterior kitchen door. I say circle to the back yard. If there are bad actors in the house, they likely went in that way. We'll either find Poppy or a way in that brings us up behind the threat." Providing a better chance to protect his fellow troopers and the woman he loved.

Will's step stuttered. He did love Jasmine. He'd once thought he'd never trust again, yet she'd managed to find her way not only into his head, but into his heart. If anything happened to her today, he had no doubt it would change the course of his future as well.

Sean slipped his weapon from its holster. "Let's rock and roll."

Will stepped onto the curb, reaching for his sidearm, then stopped, something Jasmine had said circling in his spirit. *God's always there, you know. Maybe if you broke free of your six o'clock appointment, you'd see that.* Her heart laid out for him the truth he'd half considered then never bothered to ponder again.

I guess I believe God doesn't want us checking boxes. He wants all of us. All of the time. We live life walking beside Him, not live life with occasional side trips to Him. He's always listening. And I always need Him.

He might have failed to consider the truth before, but it was the wisdom he needed now.

Jasmine was right. Without God beside him at all times, he was doomed to fail. Maybe not today, but eventually. His first turn should always be to the One who created him and saw all of his days before he was ever born. It should never be to himself and his strength. He couldn't do any of this alone, and he'd been trying to for far too long.

Sean was eyeing him, waiting for a next step, but Will wasn't going to take one without giving this situation to God. Because this time, he absolutely could *not* fail. Without a word to his teammate, he dipped his head, feeling the heat of embarrassment at the base of his neck. He'd never prayed in front of someone else, and it was different. Awkward.

Necessary.

Lord, I've been running the show for too long. Trusting me instead of You. Today, I need You. No matter what. But please, bring Jasmine and me and the team out of this alive.

When he lifted his head and drew his weapon, Sean was looking at him with curiosity, but he said nothing.

Now wasn't the time to talk. It was time to move, and the backyard was the right entry point. Motioning forward with two fingers, he crept along the front of the house next door until he could cross the narrow side yard without being seen from the windows. With Sean close behind, he kept close to the side of the house, the vinyl siding brushing his shoulder.

At the gate, Sean slipped in front of him and eased the massive wooden structure open with a slight squeak that made Will wince.

Weapon ready, Will eased through the opening, scanning the yard.

Poppy lay motionless near the patio. Stormy stood over her, facing the back door of the duplex.

Adrenaline raged, firing Will's feet toward his teammate and her K-9 partner.

While he stood guard, Sean knelt, reaching for Poppy's neck to feel for a pulse.

Everything in Will wanted to kneel beside his teammate, too, but he kept his focus on their surroundings, ensuring no one appeared to finish what they'd started.

He wrestled with the dueling needs to protect his teammates and to round the corner and find Jasmine. Every second could be her last.

Poppy groaned, then gasped. "Where'd you come from?" Her words came slowly, but she was alive.

Stormy offered her an enthusiastic lick in the face that seemed to rouse her partner fully to consciousness.

Will exhaled his fear. His teammate was going to be okay. "What happened?" He kept the words low, not wanting to alert anyone to their presence.

"Came out and struggled with an assailant. Female. She was ready for me. Choke hold."

Female. Almost definitely Dasha Melnyk. Lethally dangerous if she had caught Poppy off guard. "Inside?"

"Likely." Poppy moved to stand. "Let's go."

Sean eased her down. "We'll go. Are you okay to stay here?"

Nodding slowly, Poppy stood with Sean's help. She wavered, trying to find her balance, but she braced against the siding and drew her weapon. "I'll call for medical and watch the back door. You go in. Get Jasmine before someone else does."

That was the goal. It would kill him to know he'd missed saving her life by seconds, had changed the course of his future because he hadn't moved fast enough. He headed for the door. "Sean, take the front." He passed a house key to his teammate, gave Poppy a final once-over, then edged along the patio and peeked around the alcove where the door was recessed.

It stood open. The interior of the house held an eerie silence that screamed he might be too late.

Will peeked into the kitchen. No one was there.

Lord, help me save her. I can't do this by myself.

From the living room, a woman's voice lilted to him. "Jasmine? Come out, come out wherever you are."

His fingers tightened on the pistol grip, finger slipping toward the trigger. Dasha Melnyk was taunting Jasmine.

His anger gave way to a flash of relief. She was alive and was somewhere in the house, but there was no way to tell how much time she had left.

Hardly breathing for fear of giving himself away, he slipped into the kitchen, rolling his footfalls on the linoleum, praying the floor wouldn't squeak. He hated walking in alone with no plan, but he had no other choice.

Will pictured the layout of the duplex as he advanced. Once he rounded the corner at the bar, the wide-open doorway that led from the kitchen into the living room would leave him with no cover. He had to be ready for anything.

He forced his training to the forefront. Controlled breathing. Controlled steps.

As he neared the sink and the pass-through over it, he paused and eased forward slightly.

A dark-haired woman crept slowly up the stairwell, her back to Will. In her hand, she held a pistol fitted with a silencer. She was the same height and build as the assailant who'd attacked him out on the frontier.

It was likely his theory was right. The brothers and Melnyk had both been after Jasmine.

Will gave a quick prayer of thanks that the woman hadn't shot Poppy or Stormy. Still, it was clear her sole intent was to take out Jasmine.

Time ticked faster.

With one last deep breath, Will slipped past the small window and walked to the bar. Raising his weapon, he rounded the cabinet, leaving himself exposed if Melnyk chose to turn.

Dressed in jeans and a dark windbreaker, she disappeared around the corner into the upstairs hallway.

Will ground his teeth together. Jasmine was likely upstairs with no way out, and he was the only one who could save her. He couldn't wait for Sean to get into position.

Praying Melnyk wouldn't hear him, Will hurried for the stairwell and placed his foot on the bottom step, ready to climb.

From above, a shout, a thud, and the whiff of a silenced gunshot broke the stillness.

Time had run out.

Taking the stairs two at a time, he rushed into the hallway as the cartel leader stumbled out of a bedroom doorway. She shook her head as if to clear it and, with a calculated smile, raised her weapon.

"Alaska State Trooper." Will identified himself as he took aim. "Drop the weapon."

Dasha Melnyk whirled toward him, eyes wide with panic. Blood streamed from a gash on the side of her head. She glanced frantically from Will to the bedroom, then turned and bolted, rushing into the bathroom at the end of the hall and slamming the door.

Before Will could pursue her, there was another muffled gunshot, a thud, and silence.

For the moment, Jasmine was alone, having waved off EMTs and concerned Fairbanks police officers. She needed a minute to process what had just happened.

What had *almost* happened.

From her perch on a picnic table in the duplex's back yard, Jasmine stared at her hands. They shook with a tremor that she hadn't been able to stop. Less than fifteen minutes ago, she'd wrapped those hands around a stump-turned-weapon and had struck another human being.

A human being who was trying to kill her. One who had died moments later by her own hand.

In her entire life, she'd never hit another person. Well, other than her brother when they were kids and occasionally got into sibling shoving matches.

Her *brother*.

The pain in her chest sharpened, and she dropped her hands into her lap. If Dasha Melnyk had found her, then there was no doubt that Anton Rogers also knew her identity.

No doubt that she would have to move and become a new person again. One more step removed from her brother, from her parents...

And from Will.

Near the back door of the house, a small contingent of K-9 troopers huddled around Poppy, who had been hefted onto a gurney and was about to be carted around the house by EMTs who'd arrived only moments before. From the triumphant smile on her face, she was going to be okay.

But Will was nowhere to be seen.

He'd burst into the bedroom to find Jasmine still holding the cypress stump that had delivered a glancing blow to the side of Melnyk's head and had likely saved Jasmine.

Sean had been right behind him and had taken over the scene so that Will could escort Jasmine downstairs. He'd led her to this picnic table, but before he could speak, another trooper had called him away, to the front of the house. He'd left with a squeeze to her hand and a look she couldn't read.

Maybe he'd left already. It was for the best if he had. She couldn't bear to tell him goodbye. It would hurt too much. Because at some point over the course of the week, she'd lost her heart to him.

And there was no way she would ever get it back whole.

Jasmine shut her eyes and buried her face in her hands. She pulled in a deep breath and steeled herself for what came next. Deputy US Marshals would show up on the scene, men and women she'd never met before. They'd whisk her away, train her in her new identity, and drop her into another city and state with a whole new story to keep straight. A whole new person with a fake memory to add to her already scrambled memory banks.

She balled her fists. She could leave the program. Return to her family. Confess her feelings to Will and try to start a life with him.

But Anton Rogers would always be there. And if he couldn't make her suffer personally, he'd find a way to harm the people she loved.

No. She had to flee again. She had to—

Someone sat down on the bench where her feet rested. "How's the hero?"

Will.

Her heart rate spiked then dropped again. He might be here now, but their time together was short. She'd have to soak in what she could in the few minutes that they had.

Opening her eyes, she turned her head and met his gaze looking up at her, his dark brown eyes revealing nothing. At his feet, Scout sat panting, a happy dog if she'd ever seen one.

If only she could join him in that joy. She sniffed. They needed to talk, but she wasn't ready for the big conversation. She'd start small. "Poppy said the operation with Darrin and Keith was a success."

He nodded and scratched Scout's ear. "It was. There was more than enough at the airfield and on their computers to take them down. I had a quick chat with Eli a couple of minutes ago. He thinks there's sufficient intel on their computers to track down their suppliers, too. We might break this thing wide open more than we ever thought."

Jasmine gave him a small smile. At least her work with him hadn't been for nothing.

But Will frowned. He reached up and rested a hand on her shoulder. His touch was likely meant to comfort, but it warned her that more bad was coming. "Jasmine, Anton Rogers wasn't behind any of what happened to you. Darrin tipped Dasha Melnyk off to your new identity."

With a gasp, she sat straight up, and his hand fell from her shoulder. The cut was deep, straight to her heart. "Why?"

"Money." This time, Will slipped up to sit on the table beside her and took her hand between his. He ran his thumb along her fingertips, watching the motion instead of looking at her. "Eli found evidence that Darrin was trolling around the Dark Web, looking for some quick ways to make money. Apparently, Dasha Melnyk had put a call out for your location. She wasn't about to trust an assassin to come after you, though. She wanted to do the job herself."

Her stomach twisted. She was going to be sick. Her life was in shambles because someone she'd trusted, someone she'd loved like family had betrayed her to line his pockets. Biting her lip, she looked away from Will and watched the paramedics wheel Poppy around the corner of the house.

It hurt too much to think about herself. "Is Poppy going to be okay?"

"Yeah. She took a good smack to the head, but she's going to be alright."

"Why didn't she kill Poppy?"

Will sniffed, watching the activity near the gate. "There are some really bad actors out there who still won't touch a cop. They somehow think one LEO will make more fire rain down on their heads than ten civilian murders. I know it's a messed-up way of thinking, so I try not to dive too deeply into it."

Regardless of the twisted thought process, Poppy was still alive, and for that, Jasmine was grateful.

When Poppy and her crew disappeared through the gate, Jasmine finally felt like she could look at Will again. "Is that why you called me a hero? Because I cracked a killer in the head?"

"Sort of." He was still staring at their joined hands, and his fingers tightened on hers. "It was more because you saved the life of the woman I love." When his eyes lifted, they bored straight into hers, the message in his gaze as clear as his words had been.

He was in love with her. Impossible, but true.

And it ripped her heart in two. They loved each other, and there was nothing they could do about it, not if they were both going to survive.

"Will." His name was ragged, dragged out of a throat

raw with tears that threatened to choke her. "You can't run with me. You and Scout have a life here, more people to protect. Anton Rogers is still alive. He might not have been the threat this time, but he's acted against me before. He will again."

"Anton Rogers is dead."

The words didn't penetrate at first. They were just syllables. Gibberish. Impossible letters strung together. She jerked her head to the side and stared at the gate where Poppy had exited. *"What?"*

Two people were dead.

But she had life.

"We're still piercing intel together, but it seems Dasha Melnyk was ready to rebuild her empire, but she wanted revenge first, to prove to her rivals that she could reach anybody, anywhere. Once she found out where you were, she coordinated an inside hit on Rogers, then came after you herself. When she was cornered, she took her life." Will released her hands and laid a finger on her chin, turning her face toward his. "You're free, Jasmine," he whispered the words almost too low for her ears to catch.

But her heart definitely heard. She could be herself again. No more split identity. Just one whole person, living a real life. "It's Yasmine Carlisle."

Will slid his fingers along her skin until his palm cupped her cheek. He leaned closer. "It's nice to meet you, Yasmine Carlisle." The words were a whisper against her lips, and then he kissed her.

It was so much different than their first kiss. Now there was hope. There was freedom.

This was her real self, shared completely with him.

He backed away slightly, and his smile reached all

the way into his eyes. "I talked to Deputy Marshal Maldonado. He's the one who called me when I walked away earlier. He's working on getting your family here on the first possible flight."

"Will." Her heart jumped. For the first time in years, she felt the stirrings of hope, as though life had possibilities again. She could hug her mother and her father. Even her brother. She had her life back. She had her family back.

But Will… She bit her lip, then pulled his hand from her cheek and held it between them. "I don't know what's going to happen next. Not where I'll work or live or anything. I mean, my job is gone now."

"Well, Anchorage has plenty of freight services in need of experienced bush pilots."

The corner of her mouth lifted and her heart responded to his teasing. "Really?"

"They do. If you wanted to continue flying." He ran his thumb along the edge of her hand, the feeling both calming and exhilarating. "And if you wanted to see what it's like to be with me when nobody's shooting at us."

Jasmine bit her lower lip, partially to hold back tears and partially to hold back a smile. "I'd like that. Because I'd like to know who Yasmine Carlisle is when she's with you." She had a feeling the best part of herself could be found with Will.

"Same for Will Stryker. You seem to bring out the best things in him, the ones he'd forgotten were there."

"I guess I just decided to move to Anchorage." And probably anywhere else he decided to go.

Will's smile was soft, yet it melted the last of her icy fears. "Hey, I know you just got to be Yasmine Carlisle again, but what if someday, in the future, you decided you wanted something different? Something new?"

She blinked too many times, and the world almost went dark. Change her name again? Who would she be if she couldn't go back to—

Will's arched eyebrow and mischievous grin swept away her rising panic. He wasn't asking her to give up her name.

He was asking her to consider taking *his*.

She dropped his hand and slipped hers around his waist. "To Yasmine Stryker? Sounds like somebody had a random name generator for cops."

"Or for hero bush pilots." He pressed his forehead to hers. "Think you can live with one more name change someday?"

Instead of answering, Jasmine pulled him closer and pressed her lips to his, promising him that, even with an entirely new name, she would love him forever with all of her true self.

* * * * *

Look for the next book in the Alaska K-9 Unit series,
Arctic Witness *by Heather Woodhaven.*

Alaska K-9 Unit
These state troopers fight for justice
with the help of their brave canine partners.

Alaskan Rescue *by Terri Reed*

Wilderness Defender *by Maggie K. Black*

Undercover Mission *by Sharon Dunn*

Tracking Stolen Secrets *by Laura Scott*

Deadly Cargo *by Jodie Bailey*

Arctic Witness *by Heather Woodhaven*

Yukon Justice *by Dana Mentink*

Blizzard Showdown *by Shirlee McCoy*

Christmas K-9 Protectors
by Lenora Worth and Maggie K. Black

Dear Reader,

I cannot tell you how much fun I have had writing this book and participating in this series with so many other amazing authors. I wish you could have peeked into our behind-the-scenes brainstorming and discussions. We have had a wonderful time together!

Jasmine's story really spoke to my heart. I write a lot of books that deal with overcoming fear, and Jasmine certainly had to do that. But it was her sense of identity that really worked on my heart. We've all had those moments where we wondered who we are and why we're here. For Jasmine, her questions were complicated by living life as two different people. But, did you notice? Her ultimate identity was in Christ, and that kept her rooted even in those moments when she felt like everything was out of control. I'm so glad Christ does that for me…and I hope He is the center of your life as well!

Thank you for spending your time with Jasmine and Will. I hope you'll stop by jodiebailey.com to say hello and to "meet" some of my other favorite characters! And I hope you'll continue on with Will's teammates on the Alaska K-9 Unit. There are more surprises ahead and more clues to be uncovered!

Jodie Bailey

again, but what if someday, in the future, you decided you wanted something different? Something new?"

She blinked too many times, and the world almost went dark. Change her name again? Who would she be if she couldn't go back to—

Will's arched eyebrow and mischievous grin swept away her rising panic. He wasn't asking her to give up her name.

He was asking her to consider taking *his*.

She dropped his hand and slipped hers around his waist. "To Yasmine Stryker? Sounds like somebody had a random name generator for cops."

"Or for hero bush pilots." He pressed his forehead to hers. "Think you can live with one more name change someday?"

Instead of answering, Jasmine pulled him closer and pressed her lips to his, promising him that, even with an entirely new name, she would love him forever with all of her true self.

* * * * *

Look for the next book in the Alaska K-9 Unit series,
Arctic Witness *by Heather Woodhaven.*

Alaska K-9 Unit
These state troopers fight for justice
with the help of their brave canine partners.

Alaskan Rescue *by Terri Reed*

Wilderness Defender *by Maggie K. Black*

Undercover Mission *by Sharon Dunn*

Tracking Stolen Secrets *by Laura Scott*

Deadly Cargo *by Jodie Bailey*

Arctic Witness *by Heather Woodhaven*

Yukon Justice *by Dana Mentink*

Blizzard Showdown *by Shirlee McCoy*

Christmas K-9 Protectors
by Lenora Worth and Maggie K. Black